Praise for *Durable Goods*

"A rich coming-of-age novel. Katie's fresh yet wise voice evokes that tender passage from being a girl to being a grown-up."
— *The New York Times Book Review*

"Wrenching . . . delicately nuanced . . . Berg handles the elements with sensitivity rather than sentimentality."
— *Chicago Tribune*

"A gem with never a false moment . . . *Durable Goods* renders a pitch-perfect image of one girl's adolescence. . . . On this small canvas Berg works miracles."
— *New Woman*

"Painfully vivid and refreshingly candid . . . a sensitively told story of love, loss and growth . . . It has a message worth heeding."
— Fort Worth *Star-Telegram*

"A little gem of a book."
— RICHARD BAUSCH, author of *In the Night Season*

ELIZABETH BERG lives near Chicago. She is the author of eleven novels and two works of nonfiction.

Also by Elizabeth Berg

DURABLE GOODS

Durable Goods

A NOVEL

ELIZABETH BERG

RANDOM HOUSE TRADE PAPERBACKS

NEW YORK

Library of Congress Cataloging-in-Publication Data
Berg, Elizabeth.
Durable goods/Elizabeth Berg.–1st ed.
p.   cm.
ISBN 0-8129-6814-X
I. Title.
PS3552.E6996D87   1993   813'.54–dc20   92-28203

Random House website address: www.atrandom.com
Printed in the United States of America

246897531

BOOK DESIGN BY LILLY LANGOTSKY

FOR MY REAL FATHER

ACKNOWLEDGMENTS

An acknowledgment page is a terrifying thing, because you are sure to forget someone you should have remembered. Nonetheless:

I want to thank Howard, Julie, and Jennifer for being my family and I want to thank Phyllis Uppman Florin for being my best friend. They give me the love that keeps the engine running.

I also want to thank these people for their support of me as a fiction writer: Sally Brady and the Wednesday morning group, Andre Dubus and the Thursday nighters, Mike Curtis, Jessica Treadway, Eileen Jordan, Stephanie Von Hirschberg, JoAnn Serling, Elizabeth Crow, Keith Bellows, Fay Sciarra, Nina the Tarot card reader, my agent Lisa Bankoff, and my editor, Kate Medina. They make me laugh, keep me inspired, buy me great meals, listen to my *x* obsessing, and make me know that I am really lucky.

Most importantly, I want to thank you, the reader. I have always wanted to be in your hands. Let's go.

DURABLE GOODS

*W*ell, I have broken the toilet. I flushed, the water rose, then rose higher, too much. I stared at it, told it, "No!" slammed the lid down, then raised it back up again. Water still rising. Water still rising. I put the lid down, turned out the light, tiptoed out of the bathroom, across the hall, and into my bedroom, where I slid under my bed.

Now I hear the water hitting the bathroom floor. It goes on and on. Niagara Falls, where the honeymooners go and do what they do. There is the heavy tread of his footsteps coming rapidly up the stairs. I hear him turn on the bathroom light and swear softly to himself. "Katie!" he yells. He comes into my room. I stop breathing. "Katherine!" I am stone. I am off the planet, a star, lovely and unnamed. He goes into my sister's room. "What the hell did you do to the toilet?"

"I didn't do anything!" she says. "I'm doing my homework! Katie probably did it!"

"She's not even here," he says.

"She is, too."

Oh, my heart, aching and loud.

He comes out into the hall, yells my name again. I close my eyes. "She's not here!" he says. "So don't tell me she did it! *You* did it! And by God, you'll clean it up!"

"I didn't do it!" she yells, and I hear him slap her, and I know that next he will drag her by the arm and point to the mess on the bathroom floor. That's what I was avoiding. That's why I am under the bed. I hear Diane start crying, hear her go downstairs for the mop and bucket, like he told her to do. I open my eyes, breathe. The next time I go to the PX I will buy Diane a Sugar Daddy. I look up at the springs in my mattress. Uniform and sensible. Close together in straight lines. Spiraling gracefully upward.

*W*e live in Texas on an army base, next to a parade ground. Every morning when I wake up I hear a drill sergeant yelling pieces of songs to the straight lines of men marching, marching, all stepping onto their left foot at the same time, all dressed exactly alike, all staring straight ahead and yell-singing back to him. Many of them have terrible complexions. They sound like yelping puppies when they sing, and I feel sorry for them in the same way I feel sorry for puppies: their pink bellies, the way they do not know what will happen to them. The faces on those men do not react; they only obey. It doesn't matter that the heat is awesome, that it rises up in shimmering waves like a live thing; it doesn't matter that later, when those men touch their car door handles, their fingers will burn or that their feet will sink slightly in the sun-softened asphalt of the parking lot. On the marching field, there are no trees. The men's skin will turn pink, then red, but they will not react. Once I saw a man collapse from the heat, fall neatly out of line, and lie still. None of the other men came to make a circle of concern around him. They just kept on marching, and in a while an army green truck pulled up next to the field and two men got out with a matching stretcher.

My best friend, Cherylanne, and I play with the heat. We take off our shoes and, at high noon, walk on blacktop. The one who gets farthest, wins. Also, we make sun tea; and occasionally we try to fry eggs on the sidewalk. They don't cook through. The white becomes solid at the edges only. We call Riff, the dog who lives down the block and is always loose, to come and eat the eggs from the sidewalk. He does a pretty good job, wagging his tail to beat the band the whole time. Then we hose the sidewalk off. And then we hose each other off, stun ourselves with the sudden cold.

Cherylanne is fourteen, and she is pretty. I am twelve and I am not, although Cherylanne said this is the awkward stage and I could just as likely get better. We watch.

Our houses are connected in a row of other houses, six units all in a brick rectangle. Cherylanne lives right next door to me. When we sit out on our front porches, we can nearly lean over and touch. Our fathers' names and ranks are posted outside our doors, above our mailboxes. We have look-alike bushes in the front and the back.

Before we moved to Texas, my father came home with cowboy hats for all of us. "This is not a joke," he said. "You'll have to wear these down there. It's some serious heat." My mother was alive then and he put a hat on her first. It was white. He stepped back, regarded her while she held statue-still. Then he smiled and so did she. He never hit my mother. She was the place where he put his tender-ness. And I knew she loved him in a way that was huge, but also that she was afraid of him. Otherwise, she would not have laughed when she was being most serious with him. And she would have stopped him sometimes, like when he lunged up at us at the dinner table. Once, Diane was eating corn when he hit the back of her head, and the corn all fell out of her mouth. At first, I thought it was her teeth. I saw my mother clench her napkin, raise her fist the slightest bit, then lower it. I could feel an invisible part of her reach out to touch Diane, then come to hold me, too.

*D*iane has a boyfriend. Sometimes when they are down in the basement listening to records I hear her giggle and whisper, "Why don't you act right?" This sets my imagination aflame.

I lie naked on my bed in the afternoons when no one is home. I find a place in the sun, where the light is good, and look to see if anything is happening. Nothing is ever happening. "You should see some hair coming in by now," Cherylanne tells me. She has her period. She has everything. Nothing is happening to me. "If you want to know how it feels to have breasts, put some socks in your sister's bra and wear it around some," Cherylanne said. I did it. It felt fine. I put on one of Diane's sweaters, too, then felt myself in a line from my throat clear to my hips. I tied a scarf around my neck, put on Diane's reddest lipstick, stared into the mirror. "Why don't you—" I stopped, put some Evening in Paris behind my ears. Then, "Why don't you act right?" I said. I smiled, showing no teeth. Mysterious. "Why don't you just act right, Dickie?" That is his name. Dickie.

*A*fter an hour or so, I come out from under my bed. Diane is back in her room. She is not crying anymore. I think my father is probably in the living room, watching television.

I move down the stairs, holding on to the wall to steady my steps. I can hear the television. *Bonanza.* Good. I go past the living room, out through the kitchen and the back door. Then I come in through the front and bang the screen door so he'll be sure to hear it. I go into the living room, stand before him. Not in the way of the television. "Hi, Dad."

"Where've *you* been?"

"Cherylanne's."

He adjusts the toothpick in his mouth. "Did you finish your homework?"

"We didn't have any."

"Go to bed."

"All right."

When I am halfway up the stairs, he says, "Come here, and you can take my boots off for me."

I sit on the floor before him, unlace his combat

boots. My father is important in the army, a colonel. Men on the street salute our car. Sometimes it was only my mother and me, but they didn't know. They stopped, stood up serious straight, and saluted us while we drove past, giggling.

I like unlacing his boots. I only have to remember not to make a face at how his feet smell when I get done and take the boots off. They are to be lined up by his chair. Left boot to my right. Right boot to my left. Sometimes I say this to myself when I am showering.

*D*iane opens her door as I am going into my bedroom. She stands mute, which is worse than anything she could say.

"Hey," I say.

"You broke the toilet and I had to clean up." Her arms are crossed over her chest. The charms on her bracelet hang still.

"How do you know?" I ask.

She slams her door. I knock on it. "Get lost," she says.

I consider this. Then I knock again. Nothing. "I don't know anything about this," I say through the door. "I went to the bathroom, okay, and then I went to Cherylanne's. I didn't know the toilet broke."

She opens her door. Maybe she'll let me in. She has pictures of Elvis Presley taped to her mirror. She has a fuzzy pink rug on the floor, many bottles of perfume on a lacy metal tray, a huge stuffed tiger on her bed that Dickie won for her at a fair. But she doesn't let me in. She says, "You were under your *bed*, you little liar."

I swallow, blink. She shuts her door again. I go into my bedroom and write her a note saying I'm sorry. I sign it and slide it under her door.

Well, I lied about no homework and so I must do my math by flashlight under my covers. The long division makes me cry. First, I put down six, and that's too much. Then I put down five, and that's too little. Then I put down six, and that's too much. I erase and erase, make holes in the paper.

*D*ickie is waiting for Diane. He is standing out in the street beside his truck. That's how perfect he is, he drives a truck. I watch him from the window for a while, then come out to tell him Diane's almost ready. "Okay," he says. "Thanks." He smiles at me, revealing his dimples. One thing I love is dimples. I have tried to make them for myself by taping plum seeds to my cheeks as I sleep at night, by corkscrewing my fingers into my face during the day as often as I can remember. So far, nothing.

Dickie has on a clean white T-shirt and blue jeans, and black cowboy boots. He has green eyes and very black hair, wet-combed carefully into a perfect ducktail. He smokes. When he smiles at me, I smile back, then laugh a little. It just happens, like when you drop a plate loud in front of the whole restaurant. Giggle, giggle, giggle, like a dope. I hate myself.

"What are you up to tonight?" he asks.

I shrug. "Maybe the movies."

"Uh huh." He is tossing his keys from hand to hand. There is a square piece of gold hanging from them. It has his initials: D.M. Dickie Mac, that's his name. Once I heard Diane say, "D.M. Know what that stands for? Damn man."

She was leaning back against the door when she said that, her face turned partly away from him. She had taken his keys, wouldn't give them back.

"Come on, Diane," he said. "I've got to go. Give me my keys."

"What'll you give me?" she asked, her eyebrows raised like a teacher's.

She knows everything, Diane. She knows how to do everything.

After Dickie drives away with Diane, I ask Cherylanne to come over. I say to inspect me good, and never tell. I think there is something wrong. I undress, and she looks me over. "Turn to the side," she says. And then, sighing, "Hold in your stomach. Good Lord, if you're going to be a girl, you *want* to *learn* some things." She regards me silently, and my heart sinks lower and lower until she shrugs and says, "Well, I'd say you have breast *buds*. I mean, you can tell they're getting ready to come out."

"Thank you," I say. My relief loosens up my insides back to normal.

She lies down on my bed, spreads herself out like a starfish. "You can come over for dinner if you want," she says. "We're fixing to eat. My mom made chili."

Cherylanne's mother is named Belle. She's lived in the same town in Texas her whole life. She uses bacon in her chili, and a lot of salt. I once watched her put the salt in, shaking and shaking the round silver container for about fifteen minutes, I swear. That chili is good, though. You always want more.

Belle was good friends with my mother. Near the end, my mother called her one day and said, "Oh, please, Belle. Take her for a while. For God's sake. She keeps . . . playing her flutophone . . . for me." Those days, my mother always sounded like she was saying a poem. She couldn't do a whole sentence; it took too much air. So she would say pieces like that. Sometimes, even if you felt bad she was dying, you'd want to yell, "What! Just say it!" Even if you were loving her so much, your fists clenched and your heart feeling like it had a tight peel around it, you would get mad like that.

I had to go over to Cherylanne's house until my

dad came home. My mother didn't know I'd heard her on the phone. She just told me Cherylanne wanted me to come over. I played crazy eights with my head stuck down. I'd thought my music might help the pain.

Belle is not a friend to my father. She doesn't much speak to him. She likes me, though. When I eat there she serves me first, and sends me home with leftovers. Plus, she won't let Bubba, Cherylanne's sixteen-year-old brother, tease me; and she lets him do anything else in the wide world he feels like. There's nothing about Bubba that Bubba doesn't like. He rolls his T-shirt sleeves high up, looks at himself in every mirror everywhere, even the toaster, with one eyebrow up a little. His brain must be near worn out with making up compliments for him to give himself.

Cherylanne hates Bubba. She says he is an uncivilized being that no woman will ever love, that he does not know the first thing about elegant living. Once he hit her in the stomach and knocked the air out of her and their mother didn't do a thing about it. Cherylanne says her stomach is permanently bruised and that she could get cancer when she

16 grows up on account of Bubba. "This I will never forgive," she said the night he did it. I felt bad for her, that her stomach got ruined so young in life. She was crying a little; I could see the tears trapped in her lashes. "Oh, Lord," she said suddenly, closing her eyes and leaning her head back, "please don't give me cancer of the stomach. I have a lot of living to do. Amen."

"Amen," I answered, humbled as always by the thought that He might actually hear.

I am in bed when I hear Diane come home. My father is waiting. I hear him start to yell. She is late, I guess. No. It's not that. It's her outfit. He follows her up the stairs. "All in black," he says. "What the hell is that? A rebel or something? Are you a rebel?" She doesn't answer. I hear her door shut quietly, but then he opens it. "I asked you a question!"

"No," she says low. "I am not a rebel."

"You will not wear all black."

Nothing. I know she is standing there, looking at him straight on.

"Is that clear?" he says.

"Yes."

"Black is what whores wear!"

"You should know," Diane says, unbelievably.

I hear furniture scrape across her floor. He pushes her sometimes before he hits her. I put the pillow over my head. I live on a farm, alone, with many animals. The sky overhead is flat and deep blue. No clouds.

I am going to make Dickie Mac fall in love with me," I tell Cherylanne.

She is dropping peanuts into a Dr Pepper. She takes a chew and a swallow. "Huh!"

"I can do it," I say. "And then I'm going away with him."

"Where to?"

"Not Texas."

"Well," she says, "I suppose not. I suppose New York City."

"I suppose gay Paree," I say. "I suppose I could go anywhere I want to that isn't here."

"I suppose your nose is a garden hose," she says, inspecting her manicure. Bride's Blush, frosted. Two coats, with a thorough drying in between. Your nails tell a lot about you, Cherylanne says. A good manicure is a big part of being well dressed. Dial the phone only with a pencil or a pen. Eat gelatin.

"Well, you can say what you want," I tell her. "I am serious."

"I suppose your brain is insane," she says. "Your mind's in your behind." She will go on that way, sometimes.

"I mean it," I say. "I'm leaving here soon. I'm just telling you."

"Well, Dickie Mac will not take you anywhere. You don't even have your figure!"

"So?"

"Men don't run away with girls who are twelve." She says "twelve" like she can smell it.

"Oh, I believe they do," I say. "I have read many a time about that very thing."

Cherylanne snorts. "I'm sure. Where?"

"In novels," I say. That will quiet Cherylanne down. She doesn't read novels. I believe if you asked her what a novel was, she would only say, "a book." It's magazines for Cherylanne. She fans them out on her made bed, saves back issues on the floor of her closet. She likes the beauty tips, the romance stories with illustrations of women with their hair blowing beautifully, the advice columns, the quizzes. She likes to compare her tan with the progressively darker girls in the Coppertone ads. She is second from the best. "Your gold will always show up best next to a tan," she tells me. "The darker you get, the better you'll look in white. You want to go for the dramatic look." Also, she likes to send away for the things she sees advertised in the back pages: Garden of Eden Bust Developer, Ever Ageless Night Cream. She spends every cent she makes baby-sitting on things that don't work.

"I'm having a party tonight," Cherylanne says. "And Paul Arnold is coming." Paul Arnold, number

two next to Dickie Mac. I try to hold my face still.
"You want to come?" she asks.

I shrug. "Okay. Who else is coming?"

"Jerry Runk. Vicky Andrews. Bill O'Connell.
Gary and Tim Nelson. Randy Dreaver."

"No other girls?" I ask.

She is incredulous. "What for?"

I am under my bed, thinking about the party.
The sun is setting; it is almost time. Cherylanne's
father ordered a whole case of Coca-Cola. Belle has
set out bowls full of potato chips and pretzels and
California French onion dip. They will stay in their
bedroom while Cherylanne has the party. They always do this, at her request. "You don't want older
people at your parties," she says. "You want your
guests to feel they can be themselves, and mix." I
know it is more than that. Cherylanne likes to play
kissing games, spin the bottle. The kissers go into
the kitchen. I guard the door. So far, I have not
played. But tonight will be the night.

I push one hand up idly against the bedsprings, consider whether to shave my legs. Cherylanne advised me to. "The boys call you Gorilla Legs," she said, confidentially. And then, seeing the shame in my face, she said, "Well, they *like* you. But they have . . . noticed." I recall the nonchalance with which I have displayed myself—legs stretched out on the lawn before me in the early evening when the boys out on their bikes stop to talk; legs wet from the swimming pool, the hair (I now realize with horror) pressed flat and dark against them, sickening rivulets of water making their zigzag way down; legs revealed beneath the straight skirts I wore to school in the hopes that they made me more appealing than the full ones. Oh, I hadn't known. I hadn't known.

Cherylanne knew what to do. "Get Diane's razor," she said, "and your dad's shaving cream. Then soap your legs up good, and go real slow so you don't cut yourself. Go all the way up to the top. You want everything silky smooth, even the parts you can't see." I felt one of Cherylanne's legs. There were sharp bristles that felt like pushing your flat hand against a hairbrush. "This is not silky smooth," I said.

"Because," she said icily, "I have not shaved yet. You want to shave just before the event. And when I do shave, my legs will be exactly silky smooth."

"Okay," I said.

Silence from her, except for a short little sniff. I shrugged, apologized.

Of course I intend to do exactly as she says, except for the shaving cream part. Cherylanne doesn't know everything.

I slide out from under my bed, stand at the top of the stairs, yell down, "Anyone home?" No answer. I fill the bathtub with water, get Diane's razor from the linen closet. I will shave my legs and tonight I will dance a slow dance with Paul Arnold. Sometimes we call ladies' choice. I get into the tub, soap up my legs, hold the razor above my ankle, and begin. I feel a thrill at the back of my neck. "I'll be out in a minute," I say. "I'm just shaving my legs." And then, "Well, I was a little late. I had to finish shaving my legs." The thrill travels down into the core of me, splays out like fireworks.

I pull the razor up in straight, careful lines. It is not so hard. I relax. There are some other things

I need to think about, to remember, about tonight. Keep my chin up. Cherylanne at first advised looking down somewhat, in order to make the boy feel important. But then when she watched me practice, she said, "Oh. Well, we've got a problem I hadn't figured on. Double chin. You can work on that. Twice a day, on arising and before bed, pat your chin with your hand. Like this." She demonstrated a flapping motion on the back of her hand, a rapid up-and-down attack on her not-double chin. "You can expect results in a few weeks," she said. "For tonight, look up. And ask them about sports."

When I come out of the bathroom, I see thin lines of blood running down my legs. They are everywhere, like roads on maps. I've been warned about this. I find the individual sources and cover them with pieces of toilet paper. Then I go into my bedroom to dress. I take off my robe, check for breasts. Nothing from the side, nothing from the front. I put on a T-shirt and underpants. I put on some Evening in Paris. Then I open my top dresser drawer and take out my mother's bottle of Tabu, put a little of that on, too.

There is a knock on my door, and Diane comes

in and stops short, staring at my legs. "What'd you *do*?" she asks.

I shrug.

"Did you shave your *legs*?"

I say nothing.

"Dad's going to kill you."

"He won't even notice."

"Ha!" She sits on my bed, shakes her head slowly. "Well, you damn near cut yourself to *death*!" she says. I don't know how she can do that, swear so it rolls right off her tongue, when she is only eighteen. She says "shit" like she's saying "Pass the butter."

I look down at my islands of healing, the pieces of white toilet paper that have turned dark red, nearly brown. I pull one off, and the bleeding starts again.

"Well, don't pull them *off* yet, dummy!" Diane comes over, squats down beside me to inspect the damage. "Jesus H. Christ."

I step away. "Just get out," I say. "I didn't even say you could come in, for one thing."

She stands up, looks at me for a minute, sighs. "Come on," she says. I knew it. She will fix me.

She puts a towel down on her bed, tells me to lie on it. "You need to stop standing up," she says. "Then it will stop bleeding better." She starts counting my cuts until I ask her to stop. Then she says, "What did you do this for?"

"They make fun of me. They call me Gorilla Legs."

"Well," she says, "the hell with them."

"I'm old enough, anyway," I say.

She looks at me, her face turned slightly away in the way that she does. "How'd you like me to pluck your eyebrows?" she asks.

I hadn't planned on such remarkable generosity. I can only nod.

"You've got to hold still," she says.

"I will."

"If it hurts, that's too damn bad. You've got to keep still or my line will go crooked."

"I will!"

"All right, then." She goes to her magic dresser, takes out her tweezers. "Close your eyes," she says, and begins. It hurts, all right. But I don't react. "Left! (humph) Left! (humph) Left!" I am saying in my brain. When it is over, she hands me a face mirror. There is a little redness along my new, thin brow line. Otherwise I look good. I hold my chin up high and stare at myself while Diane gently picks at the toilet paper on my legs. "Ugh!" she says. I love her so much I want to reach out and touch her black hair. But I don't. Diane doesn't like to be touched by hardly anyone.

When Diane has finished, I stand up and thank her. "What are you wearing?" she asks.

"My black straight skirt, and my hot-pink blouse, with the big buttons."

"All right," she says, and I exhale, relieved. "You can wear a pair of my nylons," she says.

"I can?"

"Don't run them, and you wash them out good when you're done."

She hands me her garter belt and a pair of light-brown stockings rolled up perfectly and smelling like baby powder. She sighs then, a sadness in her, and waves me out of her room. I close her door quietly, to thank her.

I arrive first. Cherylanne is wearing a light-pink blouse and a pink skirt, nylon stockings, and pink flats with jewels all over the tops of them. "Well, I didn't know *you* were wearing pink!" she says. She doesn't even notice my eyebrows.

"Mine's hot pink," I say.

"Well, I am going to have to change," she says, scowling.

"*I* will," I say. "Sorry." I go home and put on a yellow blouse, the first one I put my hand to. I want to get out of the house before my father comes home. He has already told me I could go, but he is an expert at changing his mind.

*D*ownstairs, I hear the grandfather clock strike one. I cannot sleep. I feel a sweet warmth lying across my chest. I have gone over and over the events of the party. I want only to know how to work time, to make the party come back again and stay longer.

I get up, bring my pillow with me into the living room to press it against the air conditioner for a moment. Then I stretch out on the couch, lay my head against the coolness. I close my eyes, feel myself again in the arms of Paul Arnold. We slow-danced to "Theme from *A Summer Place*," moved around and around in our intimate circle. Cheryl-anne turned the lights off as soon as her parents shut their bedroom door. I pushed my face into Paul's neck, felt the bristles at the end of his haircut, smelled his aftershave, its mysterious combination of scents that were not woman's. He was wearing black pants, a plaid shirt with the sleeves rolled up, a watch, and a ring with a red stone. He danced with me over and over, pulling me closer each time. I knew he was tired of Cherylanne and he didn't like Vicky Andrews for the way she bragged, so he was mine for the night. When we played spin the bottle, he was first and he cheated. He put his hand on the bottle to stop it when it pointed at me. Then, despite the complaints from the others, he looked right at me, held out his hand. He led me into the kitchen while Cherylanne watched the door. I had never felt so mature. I stood still in the center of the dark room.

"Have you done this before?" he asked.

"No."

"I didn't think so." He put his hands on my shoulders. "First, you relax."

I stepped back and he followed me. I stepped back again, bumped into a kitchen chair, and nearly fell. I looked up, laughed, and he kissed me on the lips. I felt electrocuted. I never knew bodies were capable of this. I put my arms around his neck. I kissed him back. And then it was over and he took me by the hand and led me out. Cherylanne grabbed my arm and pulled me aside. "Now," she whispered in my ear, "you are a woman."

I was the one. I was the most important one at the party.

I run my hand across my chest. Something. Yes. I can feel something. Maybe when your brain decides you're a woman, your body gets going.

I flip the pillow over, breathe in deep. Sometimes life is so hard and then bingo, it's like happiness is pushing at your back, waiting to come out your front.

The next day, I see Paul at the swimming pool. I am ready. I have Vaseline on my lips. But he has forgotten everything. He waves casually at me, then keeps talking to a girl in a polka-dot bikini. She is wearing a matching headband and a gold ankle bracelet. I cannot turn away. I stare at them like you watch a cut bleed.

"Well, what did you expect?" Cherylanne asks later as we lay by the side of the pool, drying off. "Just 'cause they kiss you doesn't mean they love you!"

She says this with her eyes closed, her face pointed at the sky. I turn toward her. I want to ask why not. I *feel* why not. But I say nothing. I sit up and draw with the water that drips from my fingertips onto the concrete. I make a little heart, then an

X. Then I say, "I do mean to leave here, Cherylanne. I want to run away."

She turns toward me, shields her face from the sun. "Is this more of your little Dickie Mac dream?"

"It isn't a dream. Maybe he doesn't have to fall in love with me, but he likes me and he has a truck and I know I can get him to take me somewhere."

"What about Diane?"

"She can come, too. So can you."

"Why should I come?"

Why, indeed. Cherylanne likes Texas. Her father has a job in the army where he can stay put. Plus, he never hurts her. He doesn't even yell. He gives her extra money when she asks for it for the movies, tells her with a wink not to tell Belle. If Bubba would die, her life would be perfect.

"You're not going anywhere, either," Cherylanne says. "So just stop talking about it. Let's go practice back dives." She stands up, hikes up the straps of her suit, pulls down on the bottom, puts her hand petulantly on her hip. "Come *on!*" I have to come. I can't get her too mad at me. I am always on thin ice, being so much younger than she is. At school, I am not allowed to sit with her in the lunchroom or say anything to her in the halls. But in the neighborhood, I can know her.

I stand up, but rather than concentrate on back dives so I can assign them a number value, I let my own thinking in. Cherylanne is probably right: Dickie will never agree to take me away, even if Diane sits between us. But there is an alternative. My mother could come back. This thought is dangerous, something I shouldn't do, like a sin. But I fall into the luxury of it, let it have me like quicksand. I think, she could be *not* dead. Her sickness made her look dead. But then right after we left the grave site, she woke up and said, "Just a minute, just a minute, I am still alive." Someone helped her out of the casket and said, "Well, for heaven's sake, let me call your family." But she said, "Oh, no, let me rest a little and surprise them." Now she was ready, and when I got home from swimming, there she would be, making dinner, and she would see me and rush to take the wet towel from me, say, "Why, honey, look at you. Why don't you dry off and I'll fix us a snack." She would give me red Jell-O, slices of banana suspended in it like magic. She would be making scalloped potatoes and ham for dinner because they were my favorite. She would be singing in her shy voice, and when it was time for my father to come home, she would watch out the window for him. She always did. And he would come home and his happiness in seeing her would set him right. I knew rightness was in him. I'd seen it. Once Cherylanne and I were in the book section of the PX. She was picking out magazines, and I was reading a horse book, one of the Black Stallion ones. I saw my father at the same time he saw me. I put the book back fast, waited for some punishment. But he wasn't mad. He took the book off the shelf, asked me, "What's this?"

I shrugged. "I don't know."

He flipped through a few pages, then looked down at me. "You want this?"

"I don't know. I guess. Okay."

"Come on, then," he said, and he bought it for me. The only thing better would have been if he'd said, "Give me your magazine, Cherylanne. I'll take care of that, too." But that would have been too much. I have a bad habit of doing that, wanting too much. Once I kissed a horny toad to see if he'd change into a prince. I thought all I had to do was believe hard enough. I kissed him where his lips would have been if he'd had any. Then I watched him carefully. No blinding flash. No small, seizure-like tremors to show he was ready to turn. No glimmer of humanness coming to his round, yellow eyes. He stayed a horny toad through and through. Still, looking at him close up like that let me see his holiness. I rubbed his tough underbelly and he cut loose on my hand. Scared, I guess. I dropped him too hard and he ran away.

But my father did buy me that book, for no reason. I know it happened, because I still have it. And always at Christmas, he buys everything we put on our lists. Except not my mother's. On her list she would put "Stationery. Bath oil. Gloves." He would buy her negligees, filmy things the color of butter or twilight. He would buy her cashmere sweaters, ropes of pearls. She would hold them up and say, "How beautiful. Oh, how lovely," and then put them away. I never did see her wear any of those things. I was allowed to look at them, spread them across her wide bed in different arrangements when my father wasn't home. I couldn't put anything on, though.

He did it this past year, too, the first Christmas

without my mother. That part stayed the same. He bought so much for Diane and me and watched us open everything, and it made me so ashamed, that bigger and bigger pile of presents. "Oh, *thank* you," we always say after we open each one, and he nods, not saying a word. He's sorry, that's all. Sometimes he tells you he is sorry about the way he is. And then, you can't help it, you feel sorry for him. My mother in her apron, breaking off the ends of the green beans, then putting them into the colander: "You must understand that he doesn't always know what he is doing. He doesn't mean it." Her forgiving hands along either side of my face, her close and still look into my eyes. "You must understand this, all right?"

Me, taking a bean, being so bold. Saying, "Okay, all right," and then leaving a room full of lies that could burn you if they took another form.

*C*herylanne surfaces like a seal in the blue water. She stays in the spot where she came up, treading water, pushing her hair off her face, squinting in the sun. "How was that one?" she asks.

I hadn't been watching. "Ten," I say. "Perfect."

"I thought so!" she yells and then swims to the side of the pool, pulls herself up the ladder, swaying her butt back and forth, her happiness dance.

I see the lifeguard Cherylanne has a crush on come out of the changing room. He will take a dip before he mounts the chair; he always does. When Cherylanne comes over to me, I point in his direction. "Look who's here."

She pales slightly, sets her mouth for duty. "Let's go."

The lifeguard is in the shallow end of the pool, splashing water on his muscles. The woman he is talking to is wearing a black suit made strictly for a grown-up. She has a puffed-out blond hairdo, draw-on eyebrows, and spiky black lashes. She has kept on her dangly silver earrings and a bracelet. It's a cinch that woman will not be swimming one stroke. She moves her hands through the water gently, her fingers ballet posed. Then she leans over slightly, revealing her big bosom, looks up to smile at Cherylanne's man, and he smiles right back at her. I have told Cherylanne she should forget about this lifeguard. Obviously he is too old for her, way in his twenties. But Cherylanne likes older men, ever since she read some story a couple years ago about what she called a May-December romance. "What's that mean?" I asked.

"*You* know," she said. "*She* is May, and *he* is December."

"I don't get it," I said.

But I know now, and I know, too, that my job is to splash the competition to make her makeup run, to make her hair flatten against her cheeks. I slide into the pool, take a deep breath, swim underwater until I am nearly beside the lifeguard and the woman. Then I surface and swim close by them, kicking violently.

"Hey!" The lifeguard jumps back, pulls his sunglasses off his face. The woman giggles, holds her hands up before her as though they were a shield. Cherylanne smiles at me from the edge of the pool, nods. But nothing happens. The lifeguard resumes his conversation with the woman, stands even closer to her. He does not stand back in horror as we'd hoped, then swim over to Cherylanne to say, "Ah. A natural type. Not afraid to get her hair wet, and a good back diver to boot." Cherylanne's smile fades.

I swim over to her, spread my arms out along the side of the pool. "Didn't work," I say. I let my legs rise up, kick them slowly under the water. My cuts are all healed.

Cherylanne is still watching her competitor. "I hate her," she says. "She's so trashy. She probably paid ten cents for that bathing suit."

I look across the pool and see that Paul Arnold has stretched his towel and himself out beside the girl in polka dots. He is tuning her transistor radio. I turn to Cherylanne. "Let's go. We are about all struck out here."

*W*e are at the snack bar, eating french fries covered with enough catsup to be camouflage. Cherylanne sighs, pokes at one fry with another.

"What?" I say.

"I am so tired of only *wait*ing," she says. Here is why we are friends. Sometimes she says something and I know so much what she means I could have said it myself, and at the same exact time, too.

I reach out to touch her arm. "I know."

Her eyes widen and she sits up. I think for a moment I have cured her. But then she says, "Your dad's coming."

I turn around and see him crossing the room toward me, covering the distance quickly with his long strides. He is a tall man. But that's not what people say about him. They say he is big. I am confused by the urgent look on his face. I think for a moment that he is coming again to tell me my mother has died. But it is not that: he is upset about something else. When he reaches our table, I wave, say, "Hi."

"Where's your sister?"

I shrug. "I don't know. Sometimes on Saturdays she goes shopping."

He looks away, considering this, then back at me. "What are you doing here?"

I point to the french fries. "Eating."

He stares at the towel wrapped around me, the plastic sandals on my feet. "Get home."

Cherylanne has not moved. She has barely looked up. "I have to go," I tell her. She nods.

I walk ahead of my father. I believe this is happening because I am dressed wrong. But I'm not sure. I try to walk straight, not too fast, not too slow. When we are outside and no one is in sight, he takes my arm and turns me around. "Just what do you think you're doing in that snack bar?"

Well, I have answered one way already. He needs something else. "Cherylanne was hungry."

"Hungry for what?"

"French fries, obviously."

There it is, his hand across my face, the familiar sting. "Don't get smart!"

I stare up into his eyes. They are only blue, like a movie star's. And yet.

"And get that look off your face!"

Now comes the part where I must rearrange my face so that a definite change can be seen. But the change must be in the right direction. If you do it wrong, he gets madder. I make myself blank, all on the inside, all on the outside. Wrong. He hits me again, harder. But it is only on my arm this time. And we are almost home.

I am sent to my room, where I am glad to go. He told me he knows french fries are not why I went to the snack bar. And I am sitting at my desk wondering what it is I don't know about myself when I hear the screen door bang shut. Diane is home. And then I hear him start in with her.

I open my top drawer quietly, lift up some things to find the poem I am working on. It is about the beauty of dusk, about the peace of people going to sleep. I like to believe that there are no time zones, that all of us could at the exact same moment crawl under our blankets and close our tired eyes.

I am outside sitting on the porch, waiting for Cherylanne. We are going to the movies, and whenever we do she makes a big fuss over herself, takes forever getting ready. Anyone could be there: The lifeguard. Rock Hudson. A talent scout looking for someone exactly like Cherylanne, driving all around the world in his white Cadillac car until he finds just her. You might as well be prepared, is how Cherylanne feels. She'll take a double shower, wear her Tigress perfume from the bottle with the fake-fur top.

The sun is setting; I can feel the concrete beneath me losing its heat. The door opens, bangs into me slightly, and Diane comes out. Her face is still red from crying. He's been gone for hours, but she has not left her room until now. She sits beside me, doesn't look at me. "I hate him," she says.

I stare straight ahead, peel thin strips from a fat blade of grass I am holding. "I got it, too."

"What for?"

"I was at the snack bar eating french fries."

"So?"

"I was in my bathing suit."

"Oh."

"Is that why?"

She looks at my chest. "I don't know. What did he say?"

"He said I didn't go there for french fries."

She nods. "Oh. That."

"What?"

"He thinks you're going there for boys."

"What boys?"

"Don't boys come to the snack bar?"

"Well, *yeah.*"

"Well, that's it. He thinks you're looking for boys."

I am actually a little flattered.

Diane smiles. "He started that shit with me when I was the same age." She looks at me carefully, then away.

"Hey, Diane," I say. "Remember when we used to pull down our pants to look at our butts in the mirror, to see his handprints, see whose was darker?"

She leans back on her elbows, stares up into the sky. "Yeah."

"That was funny, wasn't it?"

"No. None of this is funny." She sits up. "It's not right, Katie. He's not supposed to hit us like that. I'm going to tell someone, I swear. I'm going to get him into trouble."

"Don't." It comes out before I think it. I laugh, surprised. But then, again, I say, "Don't. I don't think you should."

Diane puts her head down into her lap, her arms around her head. "I don't know," she says. "I don't know what to do."

I see Riff coming around the corner. He looks like he's just gotten up from a nap, walking stiffly, his hair standing up a little on one side of his head. He takes a few steps, sniffs at the ground, takes a few more. Then he sees us, gets a glad-dog look in his eye, and gallops over. I pet him, but Diane keeps her head down, busy with her private sorrow. Riff noses her elbow, and she puts out a hand to push him away. "Don't." Her voice is muffled, new sounding. Riff sits down, his face leaning forward, his ears on full alert. Then he gets up to walk behind her and investigate, sniffing carefully. And then, unbelievably, he lifts his leg against her.

Diane straightens immediately, her mouth a perfect *O.* Then she is up on her feet, yelling, "Riff! Jesus! God*damn* it!" She holds the back of her blouse away from her with two reluctant fingers, stares crazy-eyed at Riff, who, in his mournful confusion, has sat firmly down and now watches her, stonelike, waiting to hear what to do for forgiveness.

Diane turns around in a small anguished circle, trying to inspect herself. "Jesus, Riff! You pissed right on me! Oh, God, it's *warm!*" Riff blinks at her, his whole heart in his eyes. He wags his tail one-half time. And then, despite herself, Diane starts to laugh, and so do I. "You shithead!" she says, and Riff barks happily.

The woman who lives next door, Ruth Conway, comes out holding a cleaning rag. Belle says she dusts her refrigerator coils. "What in the *world?*" she says. "Whose *mouth* is that I hear?"

Diane stops dead. Ruth Conway is a grown-up tattletale. "That dog peed on me," she says, pointing.

"Who, Riff?" His tail thumps: once, twice.

"Yeah, Riff."

Mrs. Conway frowns. "Oh, I don't think so."

Diane shows her the back of her blouse, the

huge wet circle. Mrs. Conway leans forward to look, wrinkles her nose, steps back. "Well," she says. "I hardly think it's something to talk *that* way about!"

Diane takes in a breath, pauses. "I'm sorry."

Mrs. Conway nods, lets her screen door gently bang shut, returns to her cleaning. "What an asshole," Diane whispers.

Cherylanne comes out of her house, walks over to us. Her powder-blue purse matches her outfit. She reeks of Tigress. "Let's *go*," she says. "We'll be late!"

*A*s it happens, Cherylanne is right tonight: there is someone there she likes almost as much as the lifeguard. He is a sophomore, famous for his looks, and, according to rumors, recently broken up with his equally famous girlfriend. When the lights go down, he is still sitting alone. "I can't believe this," Cherylanne whispers. And then, "Do you mind?"

"No," I say. "Go."

And she does. She walks down the aisle as though she has just arrived, her purse swinging at her side. She slides into the seat behind him. Then she taps him on the shoulder, gives a flutter-fingered wave when he turns around. They talk a little and then she gets up and moves beside him. She gives me a hidden signal, a victory sign. I am dismissed. I watch the movie for a while, but it is only about handsome men riding around in chariots trying to put one another's eyes out. I leave.

No one is home. I make a mayonnaise sandwich. For dessert I have sweetened condensed milk on graham crackers. Then I go outside and lie in the backyard, look up at the stars. I hear the back door open, and sit up quickly.

"What are you doing?" he asks.

"Nothing."

"Well, you're doing something."

"I'm . . . I was looking at the stars."

"Uh huh." He walks over, lies down heavily beside me, looks up into the sky. "Do you know the names of any of the constellations?"

"Of course." Careful. "I learned them in school." Safe. I show him the Big Dipper, the Little Dipper, Orion.

"Some of the light you see," he says, "is from stars that no longer exist."

"Yes."

"How do you like that?" He is so satisfied, like he made it up.

"I don't," I say.

He looks over at me. "You don't, huh? Why not?"

"I don't know. It makes me sad. Like when we move and right before we go I make a new friend and then I can never know them."

"Well." A hard edge. His disapproval. He doesn't like to hear complaining about the way we move so much. We are not allowed to cry when we drive away—or at any other time, either—about any place we leave behind. Sometimes it aches so hard, the thought of all you can't have anymore, your desk the third in the third row, the place where

you buy licorice, the familiarity of the freckles on
your friends' faces, the smell of your own good bedroom. You will have to be the new girl again, the
one always having to learn things. But you cannot
cry about it in front of him. You have to hold it in,
hold it in, stare out the car windows at the cows in
the fields and the endless telephone poles and the
hopeful buildings in the small towns you pass
through and you have to hold it in. Later, in the
luxury of aloneness, you can call back the sadness to
let it out. But sometimes it has gone somewhere.
You have not lost it, just the ability to get rid of it
by crying. It will be part of you now, steal up on you
at unexpected moments. You will be watching your
team play baseball, yelling for them, and all of a
sudden feel a jag in your throat. You will be reading,
lying on your side on one elbow, and you will have
to stop and lie flat and stare into space for a while.
That is how that sadness is, insisting on a place in
you, but never quite cooperating.

"I like that there are comets," I say to my
father. "And I like the planets, especially Saturn."

"The rings, huh?" he asks, and I am so pleased
that he knows. We lie still for a while. The grass is

blue-green in the dark, rich smelling. I wish suddenly that I could have a horse standing nearby eating that grass, making the satisfying sounds that horses do. I rip some grass up with my hand, a little imitation.

"Do you like horses, Dad?" I ask.

"I guess."

"Do you think we could ever get one?"

He shrugs. "Oh, who knows?" It's not mean, how he says it. It is low and easy, from a rare place.

Once, shortly after my mother died, he was being this way; and he asked me to sing for him. I told him I would if he wouldn't look. So he lay on his bed with his handkerchief over his face while I sat on the chair and sang "Beautiful Dreamer." When I was through I sat quietly, waiting for him to say something. But he didn't. I saw the small rise and fall of the handkerchief as he breathed. When, finally, I got up to leave, he said, "Katie."

"Yes?"

He pulled the handkerchief off his face. "That was good." There were tears in the corners of his eyes. They caught the light of the sun, sinking in the sky outside his window.

I could hardly stand it. I said, "Thank you," and fled. I'd heard it, too: my mother singing, out of my mouth.

"Dad?" I say.

"Yeah."

"What did Mom die from? What happened to her?"

"Cancer. You know that."

"I know. But what happened exactly that made her die?"

There is a long silence. Then he clears his throat and says, "I am not prepared to talk about that now."

"But you will be sometime?"

"Go to bed, Katie."

I go to my room, and he stays outside. I watch him from my window, lying on his back, his arms under his head, looking up into the sky as though he is searching. I look up, too, and find the same thing: everything, written in a language we just don't understand. My mother sitting at the kitchen table, an untouched cup of coffee before her, her head in her hands. "I don't know," she is saying softly. "I just don't know."

*B*ubba has found Cherylanne's and my secret basket. Some time ago, we strung a rope between our two hall windows, over the porch roof that connects our houses to each other. We send messages back and forth in an old Easter basket, yellow and green and still smelling faintly of chocolate. We have long yellow yarn pulls on either side of the basket.

"What the hell do you need that for?" Diane asked when she found out we had built it.

"Messages," I told her, and truly I expected her to understand.

"You can't hardly breathe in one of these houses without someone next door hearing you," Diane said.

"That's why we need it," I said. This was not strictly true. The last message I sent Cherylanne had said, "What are you having for dinner tonight?"

Diane had frowned. We'd been doing the dishes. I liked to watch the way she plunged the soapy rag into the glasses, wiped around and around on the plates until they squeaked, squeezed hard against the messy tongs of the forks so that they came out clean and shiny. I couldn't wait to be the washer: so much variety, control of the bubbles. For now, I had to be the wiper. "Put *this* message in your basket," Diane had said. And then she sang softly in her flirty voice, "I hear the cotton woods whispering above." I sang back sincerely, "Tammy, Tammy, Tammy's in love." Diane was always Tammy; I was always the chorus. You can expect that when you are the wiper.

But now Cherylanne's brother has found our basket and is wearing it around on his head. He has tied the yellow yarn pulls into a bow under his chin. "Don't you *love* my new chapeau?" he asks Cherylanne. And then, "Man, you act like a five-year-old!" He has a barklike laugh, cruel and stupid sounding.

"You don't know a thing about it," Cherylanne says. "You don't know what we do with that basket."

"Espionage, I suppose," he says.

"Let's go," Cherylanne tells me, and slams out the front door. Once outside, she asks, "What's espionage?"

"James Bond," I say. "Spies."

"Well," she says, midway between flattered and insulted.

"We could pay him back, you know," I say.

"Who?"

"Bubba."

She sighs. "No, no, you can't. You can never get Bubba back. He will only do twice as much back to you. You can't do anything to him."

Sometimes I feel as if I am Cherylanne's mother. I feel sorry for her in the tender, smiley way. "You just do it wrong," I say.

"What do you mean?"

"You try to do things to him yourself."

"Well, what else?"

"Sit down," I tell her, indicating our alcove in the backyard bushes. This is where we sit in the heat of the day sometimes, watching life work around us. Cherylanne sits down, sighs. I like when something's almost lost and you are there to save it. I sit beside her, then ask, "What does Bubba *really* love?"

Cherylanne frowns. "Janie Atkinson, of course. What do you think?"

Of course. I hadn't thought of that, though I

should have. Bubba's love for Janie Atkinson nearly wears out his face every time he sees her. The only thing good about Janie, with her smooth heart face and her everyday nylon stockings and her mother driving her back and forth to school like she has a problem, the only thing good about her is that so far she has resisted Bubba's charms. No other girls have. He has so much ammunition it can be discouraging.

"Let's call her," I tell Cherylanne.

"Janie? For what?"

I shrug. "To wreck it." Sometimes things are just there, just like that. You step out of the shower and see something on your skin. You feel an unwelcome prickle moving along your arm and know that it is a live thing before you look. Here is the knowledge, so easy and mean: find what they love, and wreck it. Simple.

"What do we say to her?" Cherylanne asks.

"Something about him, about Bubba. Something disgusting so that every time she sees him, that's all she'll think."

Cherylanne frowns, bites her lip. She is wearing Love that Mango, the newest shade in her collection. The case has a little fake tip of lipstick on top.

"I could tell her that when I was five he stood right in front of me and ate my goldfish—alive."

I must be patient. "No, Cherylanne. You don't say who you are. If she knows it's you, she'll think you're lying."

"Well, what, then!" She gets mad fast when she's not the leader.

"You just real quick tell Janie something bad about Bubba that doesn't have you in it. You can make something up. Then you hang up."

She looks at me, kind of in wonder. "Like say anything I want?"

"Yes." I lean back, pull a drop-shaped leaf from the bush, rub it between my fingers, smell it.

"I could say . . . " she stops, blushes.

"It's good," I say. "Tell me."

"It's bad," she says. "It's *really* disgusting."

"Good!"

Her eyes narrow. "You know Simon LeBlanc?"

"Ugh, yes." Way too big to be in ninth grade. Creepy skin and hair. Hates everything. Wears things that jingle like the clasps on galoshes when he walks. But they're not galoshes, of course. Not in Texas. Galoshes and Texas don't match.

"I heard about this thing he did at a party." She shivers happily. "It is so disgusting I could puke right now!"

Oh, the day has turned so interesting. *"What?"* I ask.

She turns to put her head close to mine, talks quietly and fiercely between her teeth. "Don't you tell I told you."

"I won't."

"Don't you tell anyone else."

"I won't."

She sits back, lips prissy-pursed with anticipation. "Well. There was this party, and of course they were playing spin the bottle." She widens her eyes, shudders deliciously and long. I want to ask how come Simon got invited, anyway, but that will only make her take longer.

"So," she says. *"Si*mon got the bottle, and he said, 'I can screw this.' " She covers her mouth with her hand, dainty, then pulls it down fast. "And *eeuu-uwwww,* he does it!!!"

"Wait," I say.

"Can you be*lieve* it?"

"Wait."

"What?"

"What do you mean?"

Cherylanne rolls her eyes. "He *screwed* the Coke bottle!"

I think for a while. Then I say, "I don't get it."

She sighs loudly. "You know what *screw* means, right?"

I look up nervously at the windows of my house. I know he's at the golf course, but it's a habit. Then I make a face at Cherylanne while I say, "Yes, I know what *screw* means!"

"So?"

"So, how do you *screw* a *Coke* bottle?"

She looks away. "Well, I just don't believe this."

"You are the one," I tell her, "who told me how *big* it gets. You showed me, remember? You drew on my history paper how big around it gets. *That* would not fit in a *Coke* bottle."

She speaks slowly, wags her head from side to side to punctuate each word. "Well, I *guess* I *know* that."

"So what are you talking about?"

She stands up, stamps her foot. "He screwed into it, you dummy! *Into* it!"

Well, I don't know. There are some things you only can wait for time to give you.

"*Oh!*" I say, just to be done with it all.

"So that's what I'll tell Janie, that *Bubba* did that!"

"*Euuww!*" I say. "Yep. That should work."

We use my phone. Cherylanne looks up Janie's phone number. Wouldn't you know it, a lot of sevens. Even her phone number is lucky. I give Cherylanne a Kleenex to put over the mouthpiece so she can disguise herself; then, for safety's sake, give her two more. She dials the number. I hear a faint ring, then an eager, "Hello?"

"Yes," Cherylanne says. "Is this . . . Miss Atkinson?"

So professional. Cherylanne is good at this.

I hear a faint reply. Probably she said, "Why, yes, it is," and sat down with her legs crossed like she was going to win a million dollars.

"Well," Cherylanne says, "we have some information that may be of use to you."

A short response.

"First of all, Bubba Benson's real name is Irwin Edgar Hammacker." Cherylanne widens her eyes at me, holds back a laugh. I cover my mouth, nod at her. *Go on, go on.*

"Also, we think you should know he screwed into a Coke bottle in front of everyone at a party."

A longer response. Cherylanne stops laughing and hangs up.

"What'd she say, what'd she say?" I ask.

She turns slowly toward me. "You want to know what she said?"

"Yes!"

"She *said,* 'That was Simon LeBlanc, Cherylanne Benson. I was there, and you were not.' "

I have lost all my inside air.

Cherylanne is pale with fury. "I cannot believe I listened to your stupid idea!"

"Well," I say.

"I cannot believe I did." I start to follow Cherylanne out the door. She turns around, eyes wide. "Don't even think of coming with me!"

"I wasn't. I'm going out."

"I am ruined. My reputation is just in shreds starting right now on account of you."

"Well, I don't think—"

She holds up a hand. "Don't even say it. Don't even try. I cannot believe I listened to your stupid idea." She goes out the door.

I lean my forehead against the screen, watch her walk away. "It was your idea, anyway," I say.

She turns around, murder in her eyes. "What?"

"Nothing."

She walks off toward Vicky Andrews's house. I go outside, do a handstand against the wall, look at the concrete close up.

I hear a truck coming. I kick down, straighten my blouse. Dickie lets Diane out. "See you tonight!" she yells after him, then walks up to stand before me. "What are you doing?"

"Nothing." I follow her into the house. "Where you been?"

"Out."

She never tells me. "You can't go out tonight," I say. "It's Sunday." We go to the Officer's Club for dinner every Sunday night, wear dresses, he wears a suit.

"After," Diane says.

"He'll say no."

She turns to me, decides yes, tells me, "He won't know."

"Oh."

She goes upstairs. I hear the door to her room close. I wonder what she does in there all the time. It's a small room. She plays records, I know, paints her nails. But then what? I am more an outside type.

I think for one second about getting Cheryl-anne to go swimming, then remember. She wouldn't even go to the PX with me, now. She'll be off limits for a good three days.

I go up to Diane's room, knock on the door. "Can I come in?"

"No."

I slide under my bed, regard the dust motes. Sometimes they are beautiful. They are how you can see air. I think about Simon LeBlanc. Sex is so shaky and mysterious. I will never unravel it. "Mom," I whisper. "Are you there?" Not today.

*T*here are times I try to understand. "He was raised by very cruel parents," my mother said. She was wearing the blue apron, making apple crisp. She shook her head, waved her arm like she was pushing her own thoughts away. "Believe me, you don't want to know what he went through."

I think, what else? What else could have happened to him? He might have had another job, and been different. I do not believe the army is a good idea for people with regular human hearts. He could have been a thing like a janitor in a school. Everyone likes the janitor at my school, a gentle Mexican man named Juan who speaks no English but smiles and nods at every one of us like friends. He stands with his mop like a dancing partner, smiling, smiling. We have a special relationship, Juan and I. I once asked too late to be excused to go to the bathroom, and I vomited on the hall floor. Juan was at the other end. He started walking toward me. I wiped my mouth quick with the hem of my dress. I was so ashamed that he would have to clean up after me, and I began to cry and say, "I'm sorry, I'm sorry." He touched my shoulder and shrugged, said, "Hey, is okay, okay," and then some soft things in Spanish, and I didn't feel embarrassed anymore. I don't know, there are everyday miracles: that mess lying in the hall, and I felt fine in front of a stranger.

So maybe my father could have been a janitor. Or the owner of a bakery. Or of a toy store. He could have been something where he wasn't supposed to yell. I think that would have helped.

We are at the table, waiting for dinner to come. I ordered a club sandwich. I need to say more than thank you, which is not enough. When the sandwich comes, I will admire the tomatoes, say how red they are. I won't leave anything over, of course.

My father's suit is dark blue, his shirt so white against it, it is shocking. He wears a tie, sideways stripes of red, white, and blue. He has gold cuff links with blue stones in them. My mother, on his birthday, "Do you like them?" her hands clasped and held close to her heart until he looks up and she can see yes.

Diane sighs. My father raises his eyebrows at her. "You got a problem?" he asks.

She almost starts to laugh. "No. I don't have a problem."

"Good." A little too loud, but nothing will happen here. Still, you can see the sides of his cheeks going in and out, his prelude to anger. When you see that, you don't provoke him, my mother said. You just don't push him. Or you are asking for it.

They are at each other a lot, he and Diane. It seems almost constant lately. Maybe Diane is just too old.

"Are we getting dessert?" I ask, though I know.

"Yes," he says, "you can have dessert."

"Are you?" I ask Diane.

"No." We both look at her. "I just don't want any dessert, all right?"

He looks away, scowls, and nods, agreeing with himself.

The food comes. Oh, the food is here, and we can eat.

I am in bed that night when I hear Diane's door open. It is so quiet, but I hear it. I see her shadow going down the hall. She is doing it, sneaking out with Dickie. I cannot imagine her courage. I go to look out her window and see her meet him across the street. He is in the shadows at first, but then he steps forward to hold her. Only to hold her! I wonder where his truck is. I sleep a little, but not much, until she comes home two hours later. I hear the front door, her movement up the stairs, then her bedroom door shut. Then silence. She has done it. I close my eyes tight, squeeze them with relief. I imagine Diane lying back on her bed, quietly removing her shoes, exhaling a long line of air noiselessly. Her room is dark, the edges of her furniture softened by the dimness. Her eyes are wide open, and she is thinking.

*A*fter several days, Cherylanne still has not forgiven me. We are infected. She spoke to me only to say that perhaps we are drifting apart. I reminded her that we are not characters in her stupid magazine stories and there you are, I earned more time.

I read, I write poems to keep in my red folder, I take walks along the creek bed. I see schools of minnows, excited with their new lives, swimming fast to somewhere they've never been. I want to bring some home, but they will only die. And so I lie on my belly to watch them, make defective dams out of my fingers for them to swim through. I wonder if for them, their lives are long.

I take Riff to walk along the edge of the golf course. When I go into the PX, he lies outside by the door, waiting for me. In my backyard I sit close to him, watch the movement of his busy eyes, the back-and-forth movement of his tongue when he pants. Once, on a daring day, I call Paul Arnold, but I hang up before the phone rings. I lie on the living room floor, my legs up against the bookcase, contemplating human circulation.

One evening after dishes, Diane comes into my room. "What's up?" she asks.

"What do you mean?"

She holds up my bottle of Evening in Paris, checks the level, puts it carefully back down in place. "How come you're all alone?"

"I'm doing my homework."

"I mean alone all the time. Are you fighting with Cherylanne?"

"I don't know. She is."

"How come?"

"She's just that way sometimes. She just is. She's not my only friend."

I am hoping Diane doesn't ask for a list of others. She doesn't. She stretches out on my bed. "Ummm," she says. "You have a good bed."

I get up from my desk, sit down beside her. "Diane?"

"Yeah?"

"Do you ever think about leaving, about running away?"

"What happened?"

"Nothing. I just . . . Nothing happened. I just think sometimes I'd like to live somewhere else."

There is a shift in her face. "Where you're not a punching bag, huh?"

It is too bold, how she does it. It is too much out.

"I don't know, I mean just . . . I think I would just like to leave, that's all. Go somewhere else."

"Without Dad."

"Well, yeah. I think he likes it here."

Diane's laugh is like a short cry. "I don't. I don't think he likes it anywhere."

"If you asked Dickie, would he take you away?"

Diane stands up, goes over to my window. "If I asked Dickie to do anything, he would do it." Her back is to me. The truth of what she is saying is in the line of her spine: she stands tall with it. Then she turns around, a half smile on her face. "Why? You want to come?"

I once wanted a certain ring for Christmas. It was a gold oval, and you could get your initials engraved in the center. It was too much, but I asked anyway. And one day in early December, when I was looking through my mother's nightgowns in her dresser drawers, I found a velvet box with the ring inside it. My initials. In fancy, fragile script. I looked up. There was my face in the mirror, tight with happiness. I put the ring back, closed the drawer, waited until Christmas, and opened the box I knew it was in last.

"I would come," I tell Diane.

She sighs. "I'm going to finish high school, Katie, and then I'm gone."

"Oh."

"I can't bring you."

"Oh, I know."

She starts to say something, then stops. It is hard for her, what is in her face. She pulls her beautiful hair back, holds it for a moment in one hand. "You want to come swimming with us tonight? It's open till ten."

I nod.

"Okay," she says. "We'll do that."

*E*ven when Cherylanne and I are fighting, we don't knock. I go into her house, yell, "Hello?" There are the smells I've missed: new carpet and the food and the sun trapped in the fabric of the sofa, that ironed smell. My mother: "Now, fold his handkerchiefs exact when you iron them. He likes them straight."

I hear Cherylanne's bedroom door open, and she starts to come down the stairs, then stops halfway to look coolly at me. "What?" Her hand is graceful on the railing, like she thinks she's Loretta Young.

"I'm going swimming tonight with Dickie and Diane. You want to come?" This is it. If she says no, this is it.

There is a heavy moment of silence. She is wringing out the cloth but good. But then she shrugs, says, "I guess."

Here happiness must be quiet and slow. I say, "So what are you doing now?"

"Come on up," she says. She plays me a forty-five she bought yesterday. She shows me how she is now the darkest Coppertone girl possible, holding her skin next to the magazine page. She is right: she couldn't be tanner. "You've moved up, too," she says. "You're in between the best and the next-best now. In a way that's even better, because you still have a dream." I show her the new blond streak in my hair, sun-done, not fake. She says we could make some cookies. We talk faster and faster. I can feel relief in my throat like a cold.

I like swimming at night. The water, black and deeper looking. The lights making crossover rings on the waves. The diving board, glowing a pearl color, the sound of its springboard action carrying far. Not many people swim at night, and the lifeguards don't use whistles. They just say, "Hey, off the rope," in their normal voice.

Diane is telling me to dive off the high board. "I can't," I say.

"Yeah, you can," she says. "It's the same thing you do off the low board. It's just higher."

"No," I say. "I can't do it."

"I can," Cherylanne says. "I can take a running dive off it."

"I know you can," I say.

"Watch," she says, and ascends the ladder to the high dive. She is barely visible in the dark. I hear her voice like it is its own thing. "First, a big breath in, to show yourself your confidence." I hear her take in a breath. "Now," she says, "a slow breath out." I watch her carefully even though I am a little mad at her. She walks to the end of the board, pivots gracefully, walks three steps back, pivots again, puts her arms out straight before her. Her face is impassive, serious, I know. I see her take her steps, bounce up once, then dive down and slice nearly noiselessly into the water below.

"Great dive!" Dickie says. Diane and I look at him. *"What!"* he says. "That was a great dive!"

I fill up my cheeks with air, let it go, head for the ladder. Even this is hard for me. I don't like heights. My breaths get shorter and shorter the higher I get. I feel lightheaded by the time I reach the diving board. I hold on to the rails, look down at my sister in the lamplight. The lifeguard is watching, too. I wave.

"Do it!" Diane says.

I look up into the night sky, the peaceful stars.

There, that is higher. I walk out to the end of the board. There is no sound. They are all watching. I feel a slight tremor along the board, turn, and walk hastily back to hold onto the rail.

"*Awwww!*" I hear Dickie say.

Diane cups her hands around her mouth. "Do it!"

Something occurs to me. "Why?" I ask.

She puts her hands down, turns away, then looks back up at me, her hands on her hips. "If you do it, I'll take you to see Dickie's puppies."

"Do you have puppies, Dickie?" I call down.

"Sure do," he says. "Six of 'em. All little girls."

Well, there is no point in negotiating from this position. I start to come down. "No!" Diane says. "Dive off that board right now. You can do it, Katie."

"I just . . . I think I'll come down first."

"Don't," Diane says. "Or you won't do it. Just dive! Then we'll go see the puppies. We'll get them some ice cream at Dairy Queen."

Dairy Queen. Me, dressed in dry clothes, in a car, on the ground, finished with this. I walk halfway down the diving board, stop.

"Okay. Take in your deeeeeep breath," I hear Cherylanne say.

"Quiet," I say. "I know."

I walk to the end of the board, put my arms up over my head in the dive position, start to bend down.

"It's easier to take a running start," Cherylanne says. "The first time's the hardest."

"Quiet!" Diane tells her, and she is.

There are different kinds of time in the world. When you get called on and you don't know the answer and the teacher waits, that is one kind of time and it is like this. I straighten up, bend down halfway again. The water sparkles from the lights, waits. The puppies will be so cute. I close my eyes.

I can't do it. I come down the ladder. No one says anything. "Can I still see the puppies?" I ask.

"No," Diane says. "I told you. You have to dive."

"Let her see them," Dickie says. "For Christ's sake."

Diane turns to him, her voice deadly soft. "No."

Cherylanne takes my hand. "I'll show you how," she says.

I let go. "In the daytime," I say.

"You won't do it in the daytime, either, will you?" Diane asks. And then, almost forgiving, "Will you?"

*I*t happens. It comes to me. When I get up on Friday morning, I go to the bathroom and see the evidence. At first, I don't believe it. I stand so that the light falls on my pajama bottoms better, and there it is. It looks a little like South America, the outline of the stain. I go to the mirror, check for other changes. Yes, a certain softening, a more knowing look.

So much can happen now.

I know exactly what to do. I go to the linen closet and take a pad from the blue box. But I don't have a belt. I knock softly on Diane's door. No answer. I open it a little.

I can smell her sleep. Her shade is down, her room quite dark, but I can make out her shape beneath the covers. "Diane?" I whisper.

"What?"

"Could you . . . I have to tell you something."

She pulls the covers from over her head, squints at the light coming into her room from the hallway. "What happened?"

"I started." The word takes up all the space in my mouth.

"Started what?"

I look down at my feet. "You know."

"You started your *period*?"

"Shhh!" I'm not ready for him yet.

She sits up, laughs. "Well, congratulations. That's just when I started, right at twelve." She nods her head, thinking. "Mom said it was a gift, can you imagine? She was such a sap, sometimes."

I don't know. I think it's a gift, too. It occurs to me that I am standing in my sister's room on a Friday morning, able to have a baby. These are the same pajamas I went to bed in last night.

"Do you have what you need?" Diane asks.

"I need a belt, that's all."

Diane gets up and takes a belt out of her underwear drawer. "Here. You should get your own, but you can borrow one of mine. Do you know where to get them?"

"Yes." Of course I know where to get them. Next to magazines and makeup, they are what I have looked at most. And now one will be mine, tossed carelessly in with my lady underwear.

Diane gets back into bed, yawns. "You might not have it again for a while, you know. It can skip a few months before it starts coming regularly."

Well. All the more reason to pay attention. I walk carefully back into my room, on new feet. I get dressed, start to carry my pajama bottoms to the laundry hamper. But then I put them in my closet in an empty shoe box, and go over to tell Cherylanne.

*C*herylanne covers her mouth, squeals high. "You did it!" she says, and then her face collapses into pity. "Are you cramping real bad?"

"What do you mean?"

"Does it hurt? You know, in your stomach?"

I put my hand on myself. "No."

"Oh." Her voice is sorry for me and pleased mixed together.

"Why should I hurt?"

"Well, it's. . . . You know, generally, women have some pain. Not all women, of course. It's your more feminine types that suffer most. I take Midol."

I send my mind down to my stomach to check around. Nothing. But I say, "Well, I mean, I thought you meant like hammer-on-the-head pain. I have *pain*! But it's . . . not real bad."

Cherylanne moves her face close to mine. "Like somebody pushing down on you a little?"

"Yes, like that."

She straightens. "Well, that's it."

I have passed. Cherylanne tells me that a woman must treat herself in special ways on special days. I can't go swimming or horseback riding, I know that, right? I should nap when possible, and drink weak tea. And always check to be sure you don't need a girlfriend to walk close behind you when you come out of the classroom. "There was this girl once," Cherylanne tells me in her delicious confiding tone, "and she was wearing a *white skirt.*" I lie on her bed, hold one of her stuffed animals close to me, listening, until we have to leave for school.

*H*e has a date. That night when he comes home he calls Diane up from the laundry room, me down from my bedroom. "I'll be going out with a lady this evening," he says, "and I'm bringing her here first. I want you to behave."

I don't know what to say. He might as well not be speaking English. I might as well be saying, "Excuse me, excuse me, I don't understand" real slow, my face working to convey what my words can't.

Diane leans up against the wall. It is sadness pushing her, I know. "Who is this you're going out with?" she asks.

"Pardon me?" he says. The summer storm. The sudden sound of the thunder, the rolling of the black clouds.

She straightens. "I just wanted to know her name. Please."

"Nancy Simon."

Diane nods. "Where did you meet her?"

"When I am ready to tell you details about Miss Simon, you'll know."

Diane nods again. I have some questions, too. I have a lot of questions, too. But never mind.

*S*he is black-haired, Nancy, her hair pushed back hard and high and see-through. Beehive. She looks younger than my mother did. She wears deep-blue eye shadow and two silver bracelets and a black dress and heels. She sits at the kitchen table, smoking, smiling at me. There is a trench coat lying across her lap, tan, soiled at the cuffs. "So you're twelve, huh?" she asks. There is a tiny dot of spit on the corner of her mouth. I rub my own mouth to tell her, but she doesn't understand.

"Yes. Almost thirteen."

She raises her too-black eyebrows, jets out a

stream of smoke toward the ceiling. Cherylanne and I used to play dirty lady, just like that. Cherylanne's name was Mitzi, mine Titzi. We swung our crossed legs, twitched our bottoms on our pretend bar stools, drank ginger ale from Belle's good glasses, smoked pencils. We smoked just like Nancy Simon does.

"Almost thirteen," Nancy says. "Well. Big girl!"

There is a place just before they make fun of you. That is where Nancy is. I look down, think of a reason to leave.

"Well," I say, finally, "I have to do some homework. Very nice to meet you, thank you for coming."

She stands up, totters a bit on her high heels, reaches out to touch my shoulder. "Nice to meet you, too, honey." I smell her perfume, unwelcome in my mother's kitchen. Unwelcome in my mother's house.

"I hope to see you again," she says. It is flirty, like I am the guy. Of course it is aimed for my father, who stands, arms crossed, at the other side of the kitchen. He doesn't have anything army on.

"Okay," I say. "Well, have a nice time."

She looks at my father. Oh. I see. They already have.

I go upstairs and knock on Diane's door, open it. "Are they gone?" she asks. I nod. "What a bitch," Diane says. She is seated before her dresser mirror, combing out her hair. "What a whore."

I shrug. "Are you going out?" I ask.

She sighs. "Yes."

"What's wrong?"

She turns around, her eyes suddenly blank. She laughs, a small sound. "I don't know." She looks up at me. "I really don't."

*L*ater, when I am alone, I take out the shoe box. I stare at my pajama bottoms. What secrets lie in us. What perfection. I touch the dried blood. What told me to do this? What was the first step? Hormones, I know, but what *are* they? Can you see them? And if not, how do they know? When I asked these questions during our special hygiene class, the gym teacher told me to stop acting up. "That is not what we are talking about now," she said. "Keep your mind focused. You have the same problem in basketball." She was right. I am hardly ever focused. My mind is a slippery thing. Last time we played basketball, when the ball was thrown to me, I took off and ran with it like a football. It just made more sense to me at the moment.

I fold up my pajama bottoms into a neat square. My mother gave them to me. They are too small, but I am running out of things she touched to put next to me. I slide under my bed, lay the pajamas across my chest, close my eyes. "I hate you," I say. "Look what you are missing."

Her, on a half-circle kind of throne, little gold five-pointed stars floating around her head. She is wearing something blue that does not show the outline of her body. She glows. And she says back through healthy pink lips, "I miss you, too."

She used to tell me, when I went to bed at night, that I should hurry and fall asleep. That way, the fairies would come and paint stars on my ceiling faster. I wanted to see them. It irritated me that I had to be asleep before they came. But it did teach me one good thing: just stop looking, and the magic will come.

I opened my eyes. "Where are you? Is that heaven?"

Nothing.

I slide out from under my bed, put my pajamas in the hamper. I stand by my window and look out at the dark parade ground. It has a fierce presence, even empty.

Cherylanne is at the movies with Bill O'Connell. Diane is with Dickie. I have started my period and I am alone. I put a wide blue ribbon I saved from a birthday present into my hair. I climb into bed with a book. I lay my hand across my stomach, feel the outline of the belt. Just making sure. It's always that way with the biggest things: they never feel real. You have to keep on checking them forever.

$\mathcal{H}$e comes into my room later that night, turns on the light. He is holding my pajama bottoms in his hand.

"Are these yours?"

I swallow, nod. Diane does the laundry. Did she tell him?

He looks around the room, sighs, then looks at me. "You know about this?"

"Yes."

"How?"

"School."

"All right." He starts to leave the room, then turns back. "You soak bloody things in cold water. I guess they didn't tell you that, huh?"

"No."

"Well, now you know."

"Okay. Thank you."

"All right." He turns out the light. I hear his steps going downstairs.

Here is the thing: other ways are unfamiliar and, in a way, they only hurt. A month ago, when his father died, he burst into my room, stood still for a moment, then said, "Your grandpa died."

"Oh," I said. My grandfather held himself unto himself. I never sat on his lap. He never smiled. When I saw him, he would ask how old I was, and I would tell him; and he would shake his head, as though he were a little angry. That would be our conversation. He would lean forward onto his cane, groan a little, adjust his upper half, then settle back into himself, staring straight ahead. I didn't love that grandfather. And the fact of his dying made no difference to me. But I knew I needed to react and so I made myself cry. I put my hands over my face and thought of a book I'd read recently where the dog died. I was sitting at my desk and my father came over to me, pressed my head into his stomach. I cried for him until he was finished with something deep and private inside. Then he left my room. I felt a terrible relief. I stood up and shivered, like I was shaking things off me.

It is better when he doesn't touch. We are used to it. Mostly when he offers you a kindness, you only feel bad, wondering how to hold yourself, how to be now. And wondering, too, about the other times.

*I*n the morning, I forget for a minute about my miracle. But then, when I go into the bathroom, I remember and suck in air, happy-quick. I run back to bed, lie still with my eyes closed. I can get pregnant. I can have something its own self, and yet part of me, growing inside. Cells of all kinds, serious and dividing. Hair sprouting underwater. Fingers, and fingernails coming. An ear on each side of a new head, eyelids, moving legs and arms. This is too much! Why can I be pregnant already? At some time it must have made sense. At some time you were not in junior high at this age, but ready to be making your own dinner and rocking your babies to sleep.

I get up, pour cereal into a bowl, turn on the television to a low volume. I like Saturday-morning television: the drama of Fury and Sky King; the jerk-back kind of watching you do when the Three Stooges are on. I also like Popeye, though why Olive Oyl chooses him over Bluto I do not understand. Those misshapen arms. Never mind that after some spinach they can become helpful things, like mallets. The rest of the time you have to look at them, and the tattoos do not help one bit. Bluto is better looking. His character is a little rough, but I believe that in the long run Olive would be better off with him.

Once I told some GIs that Cherylanne and I watched Popeye. We were at the PX looking at records and they asked us which ones were the most popular. I said we didn't know. "Don't you watch *American Bandstand*?" one of them asked. He was grinning, flirting a little.

"We like Popeye better," I said.

Cherylanne gasped slightly, then stormed out of the record area into Young Juniors. "Don't you ever tell anyone that again!"

"Why not? We do like Popeye better."

I saw her face change around with the beginnings of a few answers to me, but she didn't pick any. She just walked away, left me fingering some pleated skirts. I didn't understand how those skirts were made, how they kept those permanent dents. I looked at them for a while, on the outside and on the inside, stretched them in and out like an accordion, and then I went home.

That was the end of Cherylanne watching cartoons with me. It made me kind of sad, because I thought she still wanted to. There were these forces. They would grab her like canes grabbed cartoon dancers around the neck and pulled them off the stage. "This can be a very difficult time of life," Cherylanne recently said. She was using her big lavender powder puff to perfume between her breasts. "Adolescence is studied by many famous people because it is so hard." She sighed deeply, then noticed a chunk of mascara loose on one upper lash. She picked at it, holding her face perfect, until she got it.

Then she started in with some lipstick. She stretched her mouth open, talked funny through it while she smeared on a creamy layer of Rose Petal Pink. "There are pamphlets at the guidance counselor's if you want to read them," she said. She closed her mouth, rubbed her lips together, looked at me. "If you want to know what you're in for when you're my age, I mean." And then, generous, "Some are right for you even now." She smacked her lips together hard, checked the mirror, stopped a smile just short of itself.

*A*fter breakfast, I go over to Cherylanne's. It is ten-thirty. My father and Diane are still sleeping. It's good when this happens. I like to run the day for a while.

No one answers when I call out. I stand for a while in the living room, then move into the kitchen, pretending I live there. I open the refrigerator door, sit at the kitchen table. It doesn't work. The smell is not right. Your own house always has the right smell to you, the one that quiets a nervous place, no matter what. I hook my feet around the rungs of the chair, look around, then hear the low sweet sound of voices being carried on the air outside. Belle and Cherylanne. I get up and look into the backyard. Belle is hanging out sheets. She carries them, huge and fragrant, in a creaking wicker basket, clothespins in a faded striped bag. When the sheets are on the clothesline, they make an inviting *U* shape. I always want to lie in that damp bed, be rocked by the wind and look up at the clouds.

I used to stay near my mother when she hung out clothes. I made people out of the straight wooden clothespins, the ones with rounded heads. I didn't like the spring-type ones, which could surprise you with their meanness. I took the round ones, wrapped them in Kleenex for clothes, and made families: two parents, many children, clipped all in a row on the edge of the basket high above the other clothespins, which lay naked and unchosen below them. I used to help peg things on the line. I liked the slight resistance you felt, the satisfying muffled *squeak* of wood anchoring cloth. And I liked the clothespins' dependability. Say you used them to hang out some towels and then forgot about them: you could come back in three days and there they would be, just as you'd left them, still holding something up, even though days had passed and it had been dark, even though you had sat at the table eating your second dessert, with those clothespins a million miles from your mind. They kept on working until you said they were done.

Our laundry goes in a dryer now. He doesn't like hanging out clothes. Sometimes it catches up to me in a rush, all that has changed.

Cherylanne is lying on a beach towel near

Belle, sunning herself. She has an alarm clock beside her—timed, I know, to go off every twenty minutes to remind her to flip over—and a fat new magazine wrapped around itself to hold its place. I want to know what she and Belle are saying but I can't quite hear. Whatever it is, it is a warm and friendly thing. I have known it. My mother and I, walking to the grocery store together: I had a sunburn and was wearing my mother's Mexican kind of blouse with the stretchy neckline pulled down like a gypsy, to spare my blistered shoulders. You could see fluid move inside the blisters like little oceans if you touched them. I carried an umbrella to shade myself. I felt glamorous, like someone a little bit famous. My mother told me about when she had to get glasses, when she was my age. "Oh, they were so ugly," she said. "Not like the cute ones they have now. They looked just like Coke bottle bottoms, and the frames were ugly gray metal. All the kids made fun of me."

"Even your brother and sister?" I asked.

She smiled. "Especially them."

"What did you do?"

She stared ahead, remembering, "Well, I cried, of course. And I hardly ever wore them. I tried to get by without them."

"Oh." I took her hand, held it for a while, turned the wedding ring on it around and around. Then I said, "I think you look pretty in glasses."

"Thank you," she said, but she was out of the moment and on to her list. "Baked potatoes or mashed tonight?" She stopped walking, leaned close to me. "Or *scalloped*?" she asked, a little excited. "How would you like that?" It was a whole thing for her, rich and satisfying, planning what we would eat each night. She worked to make things match. She clipped recipes constantly, filed them in scented envelopes, used them like friends.

I come out the back door and wave to Belle. "Hey, Katie," she says, and Cherylanne sits up, squints at me.

"Oh, good," she says. "Put some on my back,

will you?" She holds up the Coppertone bottle. I squeeze some in my hands, rub it on in the way I know she likes. You aren't supposed to get it on her swimsuit straps. "Want to lie out with me?" she asks.

Well, I don't. I find it boring, suntanning in the backyard. It's strictly for tanning emergencies. The only sounds you hear are airplanes droning, army men calling out army things, the cars going by in the distance. Ants can crawl on you whenever they want. When you lie on your back, you get a wet itch all along the middle of it; and when you turn over, you get it on your stomach. I like lying out at the pool, the sound of water keeping you cool even if you aren't in it.

"Let's go swimming," I say.

She looks at her watch. "Can't. I have an afternoon date."

I have never heard of such a thing. "What for?"

"I'm going bowling."

"With who?"

"Bill O'Connell."

"Again?"

"We haven't been bowling."

"I know, but you just saw him last night."

Cherylanne looks at her mother, then at me. In a low voice, she says, "I *know* that."

Belle anchors the last towel on the line, pulls the empty basket up to rest on her hip. "You can help me bake," she says. "I've got to make a cake today."

I shrug. "Okay." I like helping Belle. Even when I'd never broken an egg before, she just went ahead and let me do it.

"I might mess up," I had warned her, the shame already curled low in the bottom of my belly.

"Try it," she said. Her voice was as comfortable as a quilt. I held my breath, cracked the shell against the side of the bowl. The yolk smashed; pieces of shell fell into the bowl with it. I was so sorry, and feeling scared to look up, and all she did was give me a clean bowl and another egg. "Try again," she said, and walked away. She started humming. Country western was what she really liked.

"But I messed up," I said.

She stopped singing, came to stand by me. "Do you like scrambled eggs?"

"Yes, ma'am."

"Well, you didn't hardly mess up, then."

I had to keep my smile tight, so much was in me. And that wasn't all. Next she said, "You know, if you didn't like scrambled eggs, you still wouldn't have messed up. You're just learning, Katie. That's all. You go ahead and mess up all you want. Hell, I got a million eggs. They're on sale over to Piggly Wiggly."

I didn't do anything else wrong. I figured I might not. I'd been taught tenderly, and that's how a lesson stays. I can separate eggs now, one-handed. It's all Belle's. It's so easy to go the other way. One of the reasons I have trouble with math is that the teacher punishes you for being wrong. When you miss too much, he draws a circle on the blackboard just above the level of your nose, and then tells you to put your nose in it. Naturally you have to be on tiptoe to do it. He has you stay there till your leg muscles feel shaky. He divided our class up the third week of school into smart, middle, and dumb groups. All that trouble I have with numbers this year, that's all Mr. Hornman's.

So I will help Belle today. When I am done, I will try to think of a way to thank her. You have to give back. Last time, I gave her a new tin of chili powder with gold Christmas ribbon wrapped around it. Later, I lied to my father when he was looking for it. That was the secret part of my gift. He would have gotten mad if he knew Belle was teaching me things. "Something special about Belle?" he would ask. "Something better?" He'd done things like that before. And of course there were no answers to those questions. None that you could say.

We make chocolate cake, and I give Belle a tea ball. It was my mother's. There isn't much chance of him missing that. My mother used to talk on the phone and dunk that tea ball. I liked to use the phone after her, the receiver still warm, the smell of her tea breath on the mouthpiece. I wished I had someone to talk to on the telephone like she did. "Oh, uh huh," she would say, and wait a long time. "Yes!" she would say, nodding as though the person on the phone were there before her. It was exciting. When I was little, I would get on her lap and look through her apron pockets while she was on the phone. I found Kleenex and safety pins, mostly, but sometimes something good: an earring. A shiny dime. Tickets from somewhere she'd been. She saved them all, proof of something.

I am lying on the living room rug, staring at the radio, at the thin red line that finds the station. The radio is a big black rectangle with a long antenna, kept here on the floor, next to my father's chair. It is always tuned to his station. I turn it on, hear the loud sound of the baseball announcers. They get so excited. I used to wonder if they were being hit, their surprised "Oh!"s sounding just like it. "Oh! Would you look at that! OH!" But they were just watching the game, telling how it was to see it. I turn the dial, get some fancy piano music. I listen with my eyes closed. This kind of music draws pictures in my head, takes me places, acts out whole stories. Diane doesn't like it; she always makes me change the station. But when I grow up I will play it loud in my own house, open the windows wide.

Once, when I was listening to his radio, my father came home. I sat up fast. You weren't supposed to play his radio without asking. But he wasn't mad. He sat down and asked me did I know how a radio worked. I told him that when I was little, I thought there were real people in there, swaying before their microphones. There were tiny girl singers in formals, little men in tuxedos, their eyebrows wrinkled from singing like Eddie Fisher. And there were little instruments: saxophones you could fit into matchboxes, pianos no wider than a quarter.

He interrupted me. "You know better than that now, though, don't you?"

"Oh, yes," I said.

"So how do radios work?"

"Well, I . . . I think there are tubes."

"Yes?"

"And some electricity."

"Yes?"

"You have to plug it in."

He laughed. And then he told me how radios

worked. I watched his mouth move, and his eyes, so close to me now, but different than usual. I was trying so hard to listen that I couldn't. There was a bad hole in my brain. And so when he finished and asked me did I understand, I had to disappoint him. His face lost something. I could feel him pulling back in, like a turtle. I remember thinking that so much about him was unfair. And that starting right then, there was clean space inside me that let me know it was not all my fault. It's like looking at the pictures of those artists who paint with millions of dots. You stand close for so long and see nothing. You stand back one time and say, Oh.

*D*iane comes in, stops when she sees me. "What are you doing?"

"Nothing," I say. "Music."

She leans over to turn it off. "I hate that music! It's for funerals."

I move to turn it back on, stop. Later.

Dickie comes in the door, stops there.

"Come on in," I say. "He's gone."

"Where?" Diane asks.

I shrug. Diane looks at me, then at Dickie. "Come on," she says. "You can come with us."

The air has gotten rare. I stand up, pull down my shirt, tighten my ponytail. "Where we going?"

"To Dickie's house. I'll show you the puppies." She turns to him. "All right?"

He spreads his hands wide. "Okay with me."

I heard about someone the radio called up. They won something and they weren't even listening. Sometimes all it takes is to be there. I have never even seen Dickie's house. Of course, I have always wanted to. And I am going there right now, invited like a guest. Any jealous feelings I had about Cherylanne's being on a date go down like water in the last suck of the drain.

*I*t is pale green, Dickie's house, and it has dark-green shutters. This surprises me: I thought only grandparents had shutters. The lawn is patchy—bald here and tufted there—like a crazy-man haircut. There is a bush with flowers nearly given up on it, light-pink things with their heads hanging down.

Dickie pulls out his keys and opens the front door, waves us in. Diane goes first, confidently, and I follow. I am suddenly shy, and wish I had stayed home.

The living room has a gold rug, a black leather chair, a pole lamp, and a sofa that looks like anybody's. There is an empty bag of Fritos by the chair, and a newspaper, unopened. There is nothing on the walls, no curtains.

"Want a beer?" Dickie asks me, and winks.

I smile, look down, and then hear the faint urgent sounds of puppies. "Is that them?" I ask. "The puppies?"

"They're in the kitchen," Dickie says. "Come see."

Diane has stretched out on the sofa, kicked off her shoes, closed her eyes. "Go ahead," she says. "I've seen them a million times."

They are in the corner, in a cardboard box lined with a once-pink blanket. They are in their own made jumble, paws over heads over rumps, tails sticking out every which way. When they see Dickie, they leap up on wobbly legs, push forward toward him. He kneels down, holds his hand out to them. "I swear they think I'm their father," he says. He pats each head, and I am amazed to see their tails wag. Their eyes are shiny-new, and their coats, when I touch them, too soft for this world. I sit down on the floor beside them, sigh, smile. "They're so cute," I say. This is not it. What I mean is more. I want them. All of them.

Dickie stands up. "Yeah, they're cute. But another week and I don't know what the hell I'm going to do with them."

I stop petting them. "Can't you sell them?"

He laughs.

"Or give them away?"

"Maybe some," he says and goes to the refrigerator, takes out a Lone Star. "Beer?" he asks again.

And I do an amazing thing. I say, "Yes, please."

Dickie laughs.

"Can I?" I say.

"Hey, Diane," he calls. "Should we get your sister drunk?"

Diane comes into the kitchen, leans against the wall, looks at me. "What the hell," she says. "You want a beer?"

"Yeah," I say.

"So have a beer," she says. Her voice is not her own. She is in her own movie.

Dickie opens a bottle of beer, hands it to me. I take a sip, nod. "It's good." It is not, though; it's bitter. But I like it anyway.

"I'll have one," Diane says, sitting down at the table, and when Dickie gives it to her, I see this is old for her.

I take another swallow, watch the puppies. "Do you think we can have one, Diane?"

"No."

I pet one head, another rump, feel along the side of yet another leg. "Why not?"

"Oh," she sighs, tips her chair back on two legs. "It would be too much work, something like that. I don't know. He wouldn't want a dog."

"What if we just came home with one? He'd see how cute she is. He might like her."

"Try it," Dickie says. "They need another week, then take your pick."

"Shut up, Dickie," Diane says, but it is a warm thing, not what it seems.

He comes over to her, picks her up like she is nothing. "Come here," he says, and starts carrying her off. She is laughing, relaxed. I hear their voices disappear down the hall.

I drink more beer. The puppies are sleepy, arranging themselves like toys. I wonder where their mother is.

I hear low talk from Dickie and Diane. They have closed a door behind them. I actually don't mind. It is nice, sitting in a new place by myself. By the time I finish the beer, I am making plans. I have this confidence, like a good new outfit I'm wearing on the inside.

I can have a puppy. I can have a boyfriend. I can have a good husband, live in a house with him. I go into the living room, think how I'd decorate it. Well, curtains, for one thing; it is only civilized. And something baking in the oven, to make smells you can almost hold. Some plants. Some pictures we would pick out together: "Do you like that one?" "Well, of course, if *you* do, dear." Yes, and an ashtray for guests who smoke, and a candy dish, all with wrapped-up toffees.

In the mornings I would have my friends over. There would be a big blue plate of doughnuts, powdered sugar and whatever else they wanted, and we would talk about what we were going to do that day. "Well, he is taking me somewhere tonight, but I sure don't know where," I would say, and my friends would rustle a bit, excited and glad for me to have a romantic husband. Millions of times I would tell them it wasn't always so easy for me. "Oh!" They'd wave their hands. "You are just so lucky! You have always been so lucky!"

"Well," I would say, "I know it seems so."

I would vacuum with a new loud cleaner, wash clothes and hang them out on my own rope lines. I would be a mother to beautiful children I would fold into my skirts and keep safe. At night we would all watch our favorite TV shows and if someone wanted to talk, well fine let them.

I sit in the black chair, close my eyes. This makes me dizzy, so I open them again. I hear someone coming down the hall and I stand up. Diane comes into the room, smiles at me. "Sorry."

"For what?"

She leans closer. "Did you drink that whole beer?"

"Yeah."

"Shit!" She starts to laugh.

"Shit!" I say, too. It's easy as pie.

I start to march around the room. "I shit, you shit, he shits," I say. Then, confidentially, "Conjugation."

"My God, Dickie," Diane says, "look what you did."

"Oh, no, Diane," I say. "This is *me* talking."

Dickie comes into the living room, tucking in his shirt. Then he pulls a comb out of his pocket, pulls it expertly through his hair. He looks at me for a minute, then smiles. "Hell, she's shit-faced."

Diane is suddenly serious. "This is bad, Dickie. Jesus. We can't take her home like this."

He raises an eyebrow. "She doesn't have to go home. Let's take her out to dinner with us."

Diane looks at me, hands on hips. "You want to come?"

I am their pet girl. They are having a good time with me. "I can make us dinner," I say. "I'm a good cook." A vision: us at the table, an embroidered cloth in place, pastel bowls of potatoes, corn, green beans, a square meat loaf, apple pie waiting on the side. Me saying, "Pass me another beer, will you?" and Dickie saying, "Damn, she *is* a good cook, Diane!" and Diane getting, oh, yes, just a teensy bit jealous. Diane is beautiful, but all she makes are brown-sugar sandwiches.

"Let's go to A&W," Dickie says.

Well, that's fine, too, of course. My contentment is thick and lasting, like butter on bread. A&W is fine.

*B*y the time we arrive home, I am sober again. It is seven in the evening. Dickie and Diane let me off, then drive away. I regret their going, though I knew, of course, it would come to this. I stand by the side of the road, sighing. The sun is low in the sky, deep red.

"Katie!" I hear Cherylanne calling me from her bedroom window. "Hey, Katie!" Then, as I get closer, "Where have you *been*?"

I go into her house, climb the stairs slowly. She is waiting in her bedroom, dressed in a flowered bathrobe and her pink fuzzy slippers. She has silver clips on either side of her head, to make spit curls. There is a thin layer of cold cream on her face, making her appear slightly ill.

"Where are you going?" I ask.

"Where have you been?" she answers.

I lie down on her bed, stretch out luxuriously. "Drinking with Dickie and Diane. Drinking beer."

She stands still, then offers, as though offended, "I doubt it."

I shrug. "Doubt it. That's where I've been. I had Lone Star beer. I bet you can smell it on my breath."

She steps closer, leans in, sniffs delicately. "All I smell is onions. You'd better eat some parsley right away." That tip she got from watching *Miss America*, I know.

"I don't care if I smell like onions," I say. "I like onions."

Cherylanne sits on her dresser stool, regards me carefully. "Did you really drink beer?"

"Sure did." I hold my arm up in the air, let my wrist flop, my fingers fall. Say I had some rings and bracelets on; I'd look like Cleopatra herself.

"Huh. Well, I wouldn't be so proud and mighty if I were you. It's a dent in your character. It's something, once you've done, there's no going back."

"What do you mean?"

She turns to her mirror, fiddles with her clips. "You just can't go back. Now you have gone and drunk alcohol."

"Well, la de dah." I make a scared face. "I guess I'm going to hell now."

She stands up. "Since you are in such a bad mood, you can just leave. I had plenty to tell you. But now you can just forget it. Why don't you just go drink some more?"

I rise, languidly. "I think I will. I think I'll have a big, fat whiskey."

Cherylanne is painting her toenails. Hard. She is trying to act like I'm not there. And here is some blessed and new strong thing: I don't care.

I come into the house, see him at the kitchen table. He is reading through a stack of official-looking papers. "Where you been?" he asks.

"Cherylanne's," I say.

"Doing what?" He doesn't look up.

I lean against the doorjamb. "Oh, we went and tried clothes on at the PX. Then we played cards. I won every round. We ate some popcorn. And some cheese."

"Uh huh." He turns a page. "Where's your sister?"

"Beats me. I haven't seen her."

He looks up, something in his eyes, then changes his mind.

"See you," I say. I go up into my room, lie on my bed, stare at the ceiling. My brain is saying my name to itself. That is all. Just my name.

*W*hen Diane comes home, he calls us into the kitchen, tells us to sit down. This could be anything. We sit straight, not looking at him or each other.

"We're moving," he says.

Now we look at each other. We have heard this many times, and yet I know that what we are both feeling is surprise. Each time, you learn a place forgetting that you must leave it. Each time, there is a pulling-away pain when it is time to go. I have been in so many classrooms, looking out the window and thinking about the others going on without me. Thinking that someone else will take my desk and I will be in a new one. I will stand before my-age strangers, kids jiggling their knees and smirking a little while the teacher lays her arm heavy and apologetic across my shoulders. "Class, this is Katherine. She's our new girl."

"It's Katie," I will say.

"What's that?"

"It's Katie," I will say again, and the teacher will say, "Oh, well, I guess she likes to be called Katie."

I will be looked at, my shoes and my hair and my outfit and the line of my lips. Then I will be talked about outside at recess or in the halls between classes, in old, formed groups. "She, She, She . . ." is all I will hear for a while. Faces will close up when I appear, smiles will be thin and false. Oh, one person will be nice to me at first, someone who also doesn't belong; and we will sit together at lunch, lonely, anyway, knowing we are temporary to each other. Then, eventually, I will find my place. It is too hard to do this so often. Really, it is too hard.

Diane sighs, picks at her thumb. "Where are we going?"

"St. Louis," my father says. "Missouri."

I realize I don't know where Missouri is. Somewhere in the middle. And there is nothing I can put to Missouri. I envision the people there, all adults, standing in a circle, in dark clothes, their mouths open a little. The men have their sleeves rolled up, and they look suspicious. The women are stupidly kind. The land is flat and all one color. I don't know why this vision comes to me. I accept my own wrongness.

"When?" I ask, and hear the lightness in my voice, the pain disguised.

"Three weeks," he says. Then he stands up. We are done.

"There's eight more weeks of school," Diane says. "Can't we finish? It's my last year. I'm almost done."

"Three weeks," he says. His shirt is open two buttons, and I see the defeated sag of the top of his T-shirt. The light from the kitchen hums, shines down on the bits of scalp you see between the stand-up hairs of his crew cut. There is a little perspiration there, slick and see-through. I am afraid, seeing so much of him.

Diane swallows, looks left, then back at him. "Please?"

"There's nothing I can do," he says. "What's the difference? You'll finish there." He turns to leave.

"Where are you going?" Diane says.

"Into the living room. That all right with you?" His back is straight as he leaves, his tread heavy and certain. There is no touching a back like that, asking it to wait.

After he is gone, Diane sits quietly, her face blank. Then she tells me, "Well, I'm not going."

"You have to."

"No, I don't."

"You do, too!"

She stands up. "No. I don't."

She goes upstairs to her room and I follow. "Can I come in?"

"What for?"

"To talk."

"Not now, Katie."

"Okay."

I go into my room, look out the window. No stars, all clouds in the sky. I take in a deep breath, hold it, let it out. First, I'll tell Cherylanne. She might cry. She thinks she looks pretty when she cries, she has told me. "I have a lovely laugh," she said, "and I also look good when I cry. That is very unusual."

I put on my pajamas, sit on my bed with my poetry notebook. I write, "Oh," and nothing else comes. I cover my face with my hands. I make almost no sounds, crying.

*O*n Monday morning, I go to Cherylanne's house before school. She is seated before her mirror, making her hair into what she calls a Grecian ponytail. It is a bun toward the front, a ponytail in the back. When she has finished, she paralyzes it with hair spray. She centers her necklace, turns her face this way and that, bends over to pull up her nylons in the knee area. Then she stands, inspects her whole self. "Okay," she says. "Ready."

"We're moving," I say.

She stops, turns toward me. "You are?"

I nod.

"When?"

"Three weeks."

"My Lord." She reaches for her necklace. "Well. You can sit by me on the bus." She regrets herself for a moment; I can see her thinking about how to take away what she has just given me. But she doesn't take it back. And she lets me leave her room first. She is my friend; I have always known it. You can have a lot of shakiness on the outside and still know the inside is steady. Before we get off the bus, she removes her necklace and tells me I can wear it. I love that necklace. It is a gold heart, with rhinestones lined up coy along one side. Her name is engraved on it in fancy script. "You can keep it all day," she says. "But now," she bites her lip, mother to child, "this is *real jewelry*. Be careful."

I clasp the necklace behind my neck. I have seen princesses bow their head for the crown, nuns kneel down for the veil. This is better. The pendant lies in my new valley, between my coming breasts, shows them off a little. The weight of the necklace is heavy and good. It seems like borrowed things are always that way, better than your own. All day long I will reach for that necklace, I know. And all day long I will find it there. All you have to say is, "I'm leaving," and mean it true, say it to someone who would rather you not go, and little fancy things will start happening to you, *bang, bang, bang*.

*B*etween math and geography, I tell Marilyn Mayfield, my in-school best friend, that I am moving. She covers her mouth, the outside edges of her eyes slant down, and she says, "Oh, no" in slow motion. Then she hugs me tight. She asks where I am going, and I tell her. She nods. And then we are done. There are lots of army kids at this school, and so the civilian kids, they know. What can you do? What can you say? You just keep on acting the same, even though there is a bright hard edge to things now. Sometimes I think it is like dying. I always think that, when I am getting ready to move; then I forget it; and then I always remember it when it comes time to move again.

*O*n Friday afternoon, Diane comes home with one of Dickie's puppies and a large box that toilet paper came in. My mouth hangs open to let some happiness out. "You got one!" I say.

"Help me," Diane says, and I take the box from her.

"Where should I put it?"

She shrugs. "The kitchen, I guess. She's used to that."

I put the box in the corner. There is newspaper on the bottom, and I am sorry for all the puppy has lost. "She should at least have a blanket," I say.

"She's all right," Diane says, lowering the puppy into the box, and she does seem to be. She has her dog-in-love look on. She sits expectantly in the middle of the box and then, suddenly, barks. It is such a pure and perfect sound, high and ringing slightly.

"What's her name?" I ask.

"Bridgette."

I look at Diane, and she shrugs. "Dickie made me promise. He likes that name."

I pat the puppy's head, pull her ears gently through my fingers. They are something like silk, but warm with lifeblood. "She looks like a Bridgette," I say.

"You want to feed her?" Diane asks.

We are mixing baby cereal and milk with dry

meal when my father comes in. He walks over to the box, looks in. "What the hell is that?"

"It's a puppy," Diane says.

"What's it doing here?"

"Bridgette is her name," I say. "Pick of the litter."

He doesn't acknowledge me, looks instead at Diane, who says, with a kind of weariness, "She's mine. I'm keeping her."

"The hell you are."

"Dad," Diane says, "now is as good a time as any to tell you: I'm not moving with you. I want to stay here. I'll finish school and find a job. Mary Jo Anderson said I can stay with them."

"You're not staying with anyone. You're coming with us. Now get rid of the dog. That's the last thing I need."

"I'll take care of her," I say, but apparently I am invisible. There is something mounting between Diane and him, blocking the view of anything else.

"I am keeping that dog," Diane says. "And I am not going with you." I see his color darken, his cheek begin moving in and out. I back out of the kitchen, go into my room, close the door. There is a lot of math homework. And reading in geography. I open my *Nations of the World* book, find the place. I hear Diane yell, "I am eighteen years old and you can not stop me. I don't want to go. I don't want to live with you! I don't want to and I don't have to!"

Well, he hits her, of course, and now I hear it getting louder, the mess of him at her. She runs up the stairs and bursts into my room. He is right behind her. I keep my eyes on the book, start to read about exporting soybeans. "Stop it, *stop* it!" she screams. I look out of the corner of my eye and see him straddling her on my bedroom floor. He has her wrists pinned down and he says between his teeth, close into her face, "Don't you *ever*, don't you god-damn *ever* tell me what you will and won't do!" She starts to slither away but he grabs her, slaps her, slaps her again, slaps her again. I read. Soybeans. Exported. Soybeans. Exported. I think I'd better be quiet with my breathing, and so I stop.

I have been in bed for a long time, and the house is quiet. I will see if Diane is all right. And then I will feed the puppy. I don't think anyone fed the puppy.

I push Diane's door open, whisper her name. Nothing. I walk over to her bed, reach out for her. She is not there. I snap on her light. The bed is made, the window beside it open. A breeze comes in, stops, starts again. Did she go out the window? I wonder.

I sit on her bed. I do not think this is a regular sneak-out. I think she is gone. I wrap my arms around myself. I could go downstairs and look, but I already know: the puppy is gone, too.

Now I am alone with him. And I don't know anything. I go back into my bedroom, stare into the mirror. "Help me," I say.

*B*ubba comes to sit beside me when I am out on the porch after school. He nods his head as though we have been having a conversation. Then, "Yup," he says. I wonder if he has lost his mind. Finally, "Hey, Bubba," I say.

"Hey, Katie." He looks down at the ground, fuels up, turns toward me. "I heard y'all were moving."

"Yeah. To Missouri."

"Well, I just wanted to tell you, you know, it wasn't you or nothing. I can't stand my sister, is all. That's why I was . . . you know."

I nod.

"But you're all right, Katie."

"Thank you."

"You're welcome." He stands up, socks his hand with his fist. "Okay. Well, I hope you like Montana."

"Missouri."

"Oh, yeah." He walks away, his strides long and loping. Sod-buster walk, Cherylanne calls it.

Cherylanne bangs the door shut, walks past

Bubba without acknowledging him. "Gnats out, huh?" she asks and points at Bubba, makes big-eyes at me. She sits down, leans against me, sighs. "Your sister back yet?"

"Nope."

"It's been over twenty-four hours."

"I know."

"Well, didn't he call the MPs or anything?"

I look at her. "He's waiting."

"For what?"

This is too hard to explain. And so I just say, "For her to come back."

"Oh." Cherylanne rubs alongside of her neck, leans her head far back, and shakes her hair. A girl can add fullness simply by tossing her curls gently behind her. She rights her head, gives it one more shake, turns toward me. She really is quite pretty. She has a mole on her cheek in just the right place. "Want to eat over?" she asks.

"Sure." This is it, my normal life, evaporating.

*B*elle passes me the fried chicken, slaps Bubba's hand for taking a piece off the platter before I get it. "I'll tell you something, Katie," she says. "You're really going to make something of yourself. Your mother and I both always said so."

I smile, shrug.

"Oh, yes," she says. "You mark my words."

From now on until the day I leave, I will be like the birthday girl.

I need to talk to her. I go under the bed to call her. I close my eyes, try to bring back the vision I had last, the blue robe, the throne. She appears, but there is no throne. She is the only thing in a background of soft blackness. I think, well, now it's Missouri, and she nods her head. I think, this will be a new place, where you've never been. She nods again, kindness. Out loud, I say, "That's what bothers me, that you will never have been there." And out loud,

I hear her voice answer, "But I will still be with you." I gasp, open my eyes, and see her still. She is floating above me. "Oh," I say. "Is this real?"

"I am only your mother and I love you," she says.

"Oh," I say again. I am so afraid, I can't move, even to blink. She reaches out a hand and lays it along my cheek. Her touch is cool and light.

"You'll be all right," she says softly, and I feel tears come the way they always do when something is too true, when something is named by another that you felt only by yourself before. "You'll be fine, Katie, I promise you."

I close my eyes and when I open them again she is gone. I climb out from under my bed, lie on top of it. I think, I will never tell anyone this. But I will know it for the rest of my life. I understand suddenly that everywhere in the world are people with secrets too much to be told: a man in China; a woman in India, bending down at the river; a baby too young to speak. I see that things get delivered, invisible and long-lasting and created for reasons felt but never said.

Once a bunch of us went to see a man who was

supposed to be a mind reader. He was old and a little crazy, dressed in layers of things that didn't go together, gray whiskers roughing up his face, stick-out ears, long uncombed hair. He lived in a falling-down house at the edge of the army post. After we knocked at his door and asked him to show us something, he came outside with a greasy deck of cards. We sat in his backyard, in high grass, in a nervous circle. He looked at each one of us full in the face, nodded. We were scared, tittering a little. He held the deck of cards up in the air. "Now," he said. "Which one will I pull out?" We all guessed, one by one. I said, "An ace. A black one," full of an odd kind of sureness, and suddenly very aware of the space between me and the kids beside me. The old man closed his eyes, ran his dirty hands over the deck, and pulled out the ace of spades, showed us. The kids looked at me and hooted but the man said serious and straight to me, "Yes. You got the gift, little lady. I saw it when y'all was walking up here." And of course he had seen it, despite his house and his clothes and the knee-high grass in his yard. He knew.

I let it go. I made fun of him all the way home

with the other kids. Now I see how that was a bad sin. I see lots of things now, and the knowledge takes its right place. I turn onto my side and go to sleep, another mystery, really, if you only think about it.

Cherylanne is sitting beside me on her bed, teaching me to make spit curls. "You make a lying-down *C*," she says, bobby pins coming out of her mouth like bad-made teeth. "You anchor it down tightly, with two bobby pins lying at opposite angles from each other. Then, to make sure your curl will stay flat and flattering to the contours of your face, you can use some tape *over* the bobby pins. When you comb out, you can fluff with your rat-tail comb for a more natural look." Her magazine would be proud: she has memorized all this. Probably inside her head as she speaks, little black-and-white how-to pictures run by, step by step. Still, it takes a talent. Cherylanne knows just how many petticoats to wear to make her skirt the right fullness. Her bangle bracelets jangle and collide on her arm and she ignores them professionally. "Generally, you always want to look natural so the man won't know *what* you do to look so good; he'll think you just *are* that way," Cherylanne says. She finishes my spit curls, pulls her head back to regard with pride her excellent work. "Now, when you sleep tonight, you keep your pillow be*low* your spit curls, or you'll mess them up good. They'll be sticking out of your head like handles."

"What happens when you get married?" I ask. "What do you do then? If you wear your curlers to bed, he'll see."

"Well, you do it in the day, when your husband's at work. Make sure it's after your marketing—don't be wearing rollers around on the outside. That's tacky. You take your hair down just before he gets home. Spray your brush with his favorite cologne." She throws that last one in, free.

Cherylanne may be right about all this. It is pretty much how my mother did it. Just before it was time for him she'd comb out her hair, too, though it was naturally curly, so she didn't have to mess with making spit curls. She'd wash her face, put on a clean apron and red lipstick. She'd watch out the window for him. She loved for him to come home. Remembering her in her apron, the folds of it warm and fragrant with the smells of dinner, sets up in me a longing so strong I become breathless and have to lie down and close my eyes. I believe for a moment I am meant to be taken from this earth, float up straight to heaven, held in the center of a brilliant shaft of white light. It does not happen. My breathing returns, regular and imperfect. My eyes open. Cherylanne is leaning over me, saying, "Well, do you want to learn this or not? You'd better stop goofing around. "Now, this is important." Apparently miracles are over for the time being.

*F*inally, he does call the MPs and the next day they bring Diane home. My father, Diane, and the two MPs have a short low-voiced meeting in the kitchen. I am not allowed to be in the room with them. I lie on the sofa, listen to murmurs, to the clock tick, to the wind rise up and settle down again. I can't make out one word except for one of the MPs saying, "circumstances." But when they are done, I see that something has changed. The puppy is here, for one thing. And there is a line around Diane that he can't cross. They pass by each other with straight-ahead eyes. Their silence is whole and complete.

The packing boxes come. I like this part, seeing ordinary things get wrapped like presents, get taken from your sight until they reappear at the new place. You can count on some fragile things being broken; always when we moved, my mother cried a little when she found the shattered china cup, the arm off the procelain ballerina. "Why do you keep buying that stuff?" my father would ask. "Buy durable goods; that's what's going to make it." But even with the sorrow of some things being broken, you are mostly happy when you unpack. You are glad to see a frying pan with a curved handle your hand already knows. You are glad to have your own same bed back again, your old clothes hung in the new closet. You flip through pages of your books before you put them away. In the lonely first few weeks, you take all you can from your old things. Then one day the kids come to get you, and your regular time starts. Then you like to get new things again.

O n Friday, five days before we are to leave, Cherylanne invites me to spend the night. Though I have always been honored whenever she's asked me in the past, this time I am not so sure I want to go. I am almost done here. It seems important to keep things the way they usually are, so I'll remember. "I'll let you know," I tell her after school. I have no homework. I have no books. My arms felt curiously light on the bus ride home, as if they were going to rise up and off me. I had only my bucket purse, a rabbit's foot hanging sickly off the side. My report card will be sent to my new school, as soon as I know what it is.

"What do you mean you have to let me know?" Cherylanne asks.

I shrug. "I don't know."

"Well," she says, "I could make other plans, you know. A lot of other ones. I turned down plenty of people in school today. I could have gone out in a car."

I look at her, check for lies. This seems true enough. "Okay," I say. "I'll be over after dinner."

"We'll do the Ouija board," she says. "We can stay up all night and inquire of the oracle."

I go into the kitchen, open the cupboard for a snack. Oreos. A handful is six. You fill the milk glass three quarters up, dunk one cookie, eat the next one dry. In the cardboard box, the puppy is sleeping. Diane has been coming home from school to let her out, and my father has not complained one time about her.

I go into my room, lie on my back, contemplate the ceiling. There are some good things about being in a new place. You have to remember where the bathroom is every time you need to go, and that is interesting. You sit in your new kitchen, looking around for fun. You notice. You have an edginess in you, like when you are waiting to be called on to read the long poem you were supposed to memorize. You are waiting for your new life to happen.

Downstairs, I hear the back door open. Diane. I come down to see if I can help with the puppy. But it is not Diane, it is my father. I stop short when I see him. He has not seen me. I can go back upstairs, free. He bends over the cardboard box, looks at the puppy. His face is plain and clean, like it is resting. He reaches out a hand, pets the dog, says words to her in a voice too low for me to hear. Then he sighs, stands up, hands on hips. When he sees me, he drops his hands, straightens, nods. "Has that dog been out?"

"No, Diane does it when she comes home."

He nods again.

"How come you're home?" I ask.

He sits at the table. "Why? Are you about to get caught doing something?"

"No." Well, this could be a joke, him warming up. I sit at the table with him, finger the embroidery on the tablecloth. On the sofa, shoulder to shoulder with my mother, laying out colors of floss before she began this. The light coming in through the window at a four o'clock angle. I suggested deep pink, an apple green, a dark yellow, and she used every one.

"I've invited Nancy over for dinner tonight," he says. "Would you like to join us?"

"Can't," I say. "I'm going to spend the night with Cherylanne and I'm eating with her, too." I hope Belle won't mind.

He unbuttons his top button. "Get me down one of those cans of Vienna sausages, will you?"

We are going to have a little party, refreshments. I get out the can, ask if I can open it. I like turning the church key, seeing the little sausages all lined up like eager kids saying, "Pick me!" I am almost through when my finger slips down onto the edge of the can. I know I am bad cut because I see so much blood, but I can feel nothing. I hold my hand over the sink. It's the pointer finger on my right hand. I won't be able to write, I think. I won't be able to do my homework. And then I remember I have none.

I touch the top of my finger, and it wiggles. It looks as though it's ready to fall off. "Dad," I say, and then I start to hurt.

He leaps up when he sees the blood, grabs a kitchen towel and wraps it around my hand. "Sit down," he says. He unwraps the towel, whistles low, looks up at me. "Does it hurt?"

I nod.

"Yeah." He wraps it back up, goes to the cupboard, gets out his whiskey. He pours some in a coffee cup, hands it to me. "Drink this."

I look up at him, unsure. "This?"

"It'll help," he says. "You're pale. You need stitches. I'm going to have to bring you into the dispensary."

I take a drink, shudder big. I feel a wave of nausea, shudder it away, stand up. "Okay," I say, "let's go." He crosses his arms over his chest, smiles. At last I have done something right.

Cherylanne has rollers in her hair, a black net around it. I have six sutures in my finger, a white Band-Aid around it, serious and medical looking. "Who do you think I'll marry?" Cherylanne asks the Ouija board and happy-sighs.

"Wait," I say.

She looks up, irritated. "What? Now look, now you have gone and wrecked the mood and it won't answer."

"I want to know what you mean. Like, are you looking for a name?"

"Well, *I* don't know," she says. "You don't ask questions you already know the answers for. What is the point of a Ouija board if you already know?" She sighs, leans back. "I don't think you're the one to do this with. Let's do you a make-over."

The sting of her insult is overtaken by my stubborn excitement at getting a make-over. I don't know why. Cherylanne has given me make-overs before, and every time we get to the end, there is just my plain old face hanging out, breaking through all the tricks. Not that Cherylanne sees that. She thinks she is Makeup Queen of the Universe. She tells me about mistakes she sees on the stars when we go to the movies. "See, she has the wrong kind of eyes for that type of shadow," Cherylanne whispered to me once—about Elizabeth Taylor! Like the movie people are just sitting around the set all sad, doing the best they can until Cherylanne can get there.

I sit down on her dressing-table chair, look at myself in the mirror. One time she did manage to cover up a lot of freckles. She ties a scarf around my head to hold my hair back, and then spreads on a layer of cold cream to remove the damage of every-day living. Much of the dirt on your face is micro-scopic, Cherylanne says. She says if you could see your skin under the microscope you'd about throw up. I don't believe anything under the microscope would make me throw up. That would be like mak-ing fun of someone's house when they invite you over. Looking at things so close up, that's a modern privilege, and you owe what you see some respect.

"Now you just relax," Cherylanne says in her makeup lady voice, "and I'll be right back." It's a too-slow voice, like she's talking to someone stupid, or a dog. She puts her robe over her yellow pedal pushers and matching blouse, ties it tight and effi-cient. Now she will go into the bathroom and make her selections for transforming me. I will be turned away from the mirror. I can't look until she's all done, and then I'm supposed to nearly pass out with pleasure. I have figured out the number of compli-ments I have to say to keep her from being mad:

four. Of course, more are always welcome. She likes best when I ask for tips on doing it myself. Then she can rattle off some prepared beauty speech like the Gettysburg Address.

Well, I don't mind any of this so much, especially since at the end I get to have my hair done, and Cherylanne does it so gentle. She makes me a French twist with two spit curls, and I am happy it takes a long time for her to get it right. It is so relaxing to have someone do your hair. It is near to a tickle, without the torture. You close your eyes, and all in the world you hear is a blurry voice asking you for a bobby pin every now and then. Your brain is near asleep. You lean into those slow, fixing hands and you feel so good you could be Doris Day on the French Riviera, wearing your one-thousand-dollar white bikini, Rock Hudson leaping up to get you lemonade. "How's this, darling?" "Oh, fine, Rock." "Well, good, darling."

When Cherylanne is done, I have to sit up straight while she takes my picture. She always takes pictures of her work. She keeps them in a special scrapbook decorated with pictures of makeup products: compacts and lipsticks and creams and blush and brushes and pencils float across the cover. So far I am her only customer. I wonder who she will do when I move, and the question is like a pin in the balloon.

"Okay, you can turn around and look," she says. Well, I have on two-tone green eyeshadow and bright-red lipstick. My eyebrows are black and long as the Mississippi. My blusher looks like a twin slap. Obviously, Cherylanne is having an off day.

"Well," I say. "It's good." One. "I really like the dark-green color." Two. "I could pass for twenty." Three. And then, I can't help it, I say, "But I sort of look like a stop-and-go light."

"Well," she says, "you don't know fashion at all. This is the English look, and it's very popular." She begins untying her robe, the flush of her displeasure moving into her cheeks. "Whether you can appreciate it or not," she says, a little under her breath like she is having a conversation with herself, "I have a real gift. I can bring out the best in everyone. I do my mother's makeup every time she needs to look good."

"I didn't say you don't," I say. "I know you're good. Just, sometimes I have to get used to it."

She is on her bed, looking away from me. Then, turning back, she says, "I mean, look at those spit curls. Exactly alike."

"I know," I say. "That's what I mean. I know you're good."

She is silent, staring now at her feet. White sneakers, yellow pom-poms on them. Then she looks up and asks me, "Do you think you'll ever come back here?"

I wait a while, then tell her what I know is the truth. No. We don't do that ever, go back. You remember a place for a while, and then it fades like you're going blind, and then you start making it up. You know you're getting things wrong, but you make it up to not lose it all. And it's like the places want to try, too. They jump into your head, a scene every now and then, like the too-bright light of a camera: your hallway, here, *flash:* don't forget. The line of bushes in your front yard, here, *flash:* don't forget. All of it fails. All of it fades.

"Well," Cherylanne sighs. "Do you want some angel food cake?" Sometimes it seems to me that the only thing in the world is people just trying.

*W*e are in Cherylanne's bed, our voices drunk sounding, showing how near to sleep we are. "The man puts it in the hole and moves it around," Cherylanne is patiently explaining. "When he does it long enough, sperm sprays out. And that's what makes the baby."

"That makes me puke," I say.

There is a long pause, and after a yawn Cherylanne says, "Sex is a beautiful mystery you can't understand until you do it with the one you love."

Well, it sounds to me like the man has all the fun. The woman must just lie there, thinking about what to make for dinner the next day, and the man moves it around until he gets some sperm out, which, according to everything, he enjoys quite a lot. And all this done pure naked, everything hanging out and unprotected! How would you ever be comfortable? How could you not be embarrassed forever? And then the next morning, the man right there, knowing everything that happened the night before.

"Do you really think you'll like it?" I ask. "Marybeth Harris says it hurts like crazy for the woman. Her cousin did it and told her everything. She *bled* from down there, and it wasn't the curse, it was just from getting hurt!" Silence. "Can you imagine?"

Nothing. I rise up on one elbow, look down into her face. Her breathing is deep and regular, her own and private. I look at her eyelashes, long and curled slightly upward, the pretty shape of her mouth. I would like to wake her up and give her a big present. I hope she will find the right husband. Lately she wants a veterinarian.

I get out of bed, pull the sheet up over her. Everyone in her house is sleeping, and I feel the quiet over me like clothes. Outside, the clouds could be gauze pulled thin across the stars, and the moon is near-transparent, as though someone tried to erase it. Cherylanne's window faces the parade ground just as mine does, but the angle, of course, is not the same. It can be so different to be only next door.

Once Cherylanne and I fell in a river together. We were walking at the edge of the bank, picking flowers. She slipped in some mud, and all of a sudden there was her surprised and scared face sticking out of the muddy water. "Get out of there!" I said.

And she yelled, drifting along in the current, "I can't! I can't!" I ran along beside her, reached out my hand, and when she grabbed hold of it, I fell in, too. We held on to each other and worked to keep our heads up. I yelled for help once, but it embarrassed me and, anyway, there was no one around. I don't know what happened—the current shifted, maybe—but we were suddenly propelled straight toward the shore, and we were able to get out. I'd lost a shoe, and Cherylanne had ripped off some nails trying to grab on to things she passed. Otherwise, we were only wet. We laughed, but it was with our eyeballs wide around. When we got home, we went to my house first. My father asked what happened to us and I told him. I was a little bit proud. First he shook his head, disgusted. Then, "What were you doing by that river?" he asked. "What have I told you about that goddamn river? You had no business down there!" I stood wet and embarrassed and I felt more than heard Cherylanne leave. Later, I went to her house and threw up. Belle called my father, saying, "She's sick. She's in shock. These girls could have drowned! Don't you know that?" He gave a long answer, and Belle said nothing and then she hung up. She turned around to look at me, her eyes soft and sorry, and I wanted more than anything for her just to be quiet, not to tell me things I already knew and could do nothing about. And she was quiet. She walked away, made us some peanut butter cookies. At school the next day, Cherylanne and I told everyone how close we came to dying, how we swam out of the clutches of death in the nick of time and if they thought that was easy they were crazy.

I sit down at Cherylanne's dresser, barely make out the outline of my head in the mirror. I put my hand out, search for a bottle of her perfume, find one, put some on my wrist. It's the one that smells like baby powder and has an exclamation after its name, it is so happy about itself. I find her brush, pull it through my hair, see the beautiful blue sparks of electricity fly out. Cherylanne has a pink plastic lipstick holder, swirled with white like marble. It is filled with six tubes of lipstick, all in order according to shade. Barely There is the first one. I feel for the middle one, put some on. I cross one leg over the other, swing it, rub my lips together good. Her jewelry box is on the far right, with her many necklaces and rings and bracelets and pins. I start to reach for the jewelry box, then stop. I am me and I live next door.

I want suddenly to be in my own room, with my faded blue sheets, with my cigar box full of dried flowers and horse chestnuts and the fragile bird's nest I found at the base of a tree. A cat was hanging over that nest, evil coming out its eyes like headlights. I think about writing a note to Cherylanne, but it is too dark and, anyway, what would I say? She will forgive this; we were done with the best part of the sleep-over.

I tiptoe down the stairs, close the door quietly behind me. The key to our house is under the mat, and I slide it noiselessly into place, let myself in. I feel like a new person in my own living room. Say I were a thief, I think: what would I take? I would want the grandfather clock, the rocking chair. I would want the pillows on the sofa and the sofa, too. I would want the coffee table, the magazines on it, the sweet potato plant my mother started on the kitchen windowsill that now has overtaken the table at the side of the sofa. I would want the curtains, the air conditioner, the radio next to my father's chair.

I would want the floors, the ceiling, the pattern of the shadows made by the setting sun. The Egyptians had a good idea—take it with you. Get buried with all you can, just in case.

I sit on the sofa, breathe in deep. I am not tired at all. I believe I will stay up all night, something I have never done but have always wanted to do. At some point, day and night are exactly equal. I want to see when it is neither one.

I do fall asleep, though, because a noise outside wakes me. I sit up straight and extra-alive. There is the screen door, then a slight creak as the front door opens. This is a real thief, and here I am sitting right in his aim. I swallow, bite my lips. "Don't think about taking anything," I will say. "I am right here, with a gun." Then I will yell for my father, loud. I am a little worried about this part. In dreams, whenever I need to yell, nothing comes out.

But it is only Diane. She is on tiptoe, moving slowly toward the staircase. "Hey, Diane," I whisper.

She stops in her tracks, grabs her chest, spins around. "What are you *do*ing?" she asks. "What are you doing?"

"Shhhhhh!" I say.

"Never mind! You scared me to death!"

I shrug. "Sorry."

"What are you doing down here?" she whispers.

"What are *you* doing?"

She comes closer, sits down beside me. "Well, what do you think?" She sighs, shakes off the last of her scare. The clock strikes three.

"I guess you're sneaking in again," I say. "You haven't gotten caught one time." Three o'clock in the morning, and she's coming home! You can't help but admire Diane.

She leans her head back, undoes her ponytail holder, shakes out her hair, and then looks at me, thinking something over. Then, "I'm just here to pack. I'm leaving again, Katie. I'm not coming back this time."

I start to laugh. This is too familiar. And it doesn't work. "You can't."

"We're leaving right now for Mexico. Dickie went to get his things. He'll be back in about twenty minutes." Her whisper is so quiet but it seems to me to echo around the room.

"Oh," I say. And then, "I won't tell."

"I know you won't." She pushes my hair back from my face. "Will you be all right?"

"Yeah!" It is too quick. We have both heard it.

"Why don't you come?" she asks. "Go pack some things; I'll take you with me. I'll take care of you. I'm going to get a job down there. It's cheap to live. Come on, you can come."

"I can't," I say.

"Yes, you can."

"I don't think so."

"Well," she says, "I'm going. I've got to pack."

I watch her go upstairs, and then I go up to pack, too. Sometimes these things happen. You are walking along with only your legs saying where to go.

I creep into my room, turn on the light, find my suitcase at the back of my closet. I put it on my bed, open it. Then I stand still, listen. How can he sleep?

I put in some underwear, a clean pair of jeans, three tops. What else? I put in my toothbrush, a hairbrush, some barrettes, my mother's perfume, my poetry notebook, and the book I am reading. But then, since it is from the library, I take it out.

Mexico! I believe it is orange and yellow there, the good smell of corn in the air. We will live in a house made of stone, with multicolored rugs and a fireplace stove. We will have lots of silver bracelets. Dickie will work and Diane will keep the house and I will go to school and speak Spanish. Whenever our Mexican phone rings, it will be a fresh new friend.

I hear Diane leaving her room, and come out into the hall to meet her. "I'm coming," I whisper. She puts her finger to her lips, nods, points downstairs. Yes. I will meet her there. We are experts now at something we've never done. I go into my room to close my suitcase, then turn out my light. I feel a kind of excitement in me that seems false, like scary-movie excitement, when your heart is crying out and your brain is saying this is just fake so why don't you relax. I think, this is the last time I will be in this room, forever. I think, I didn't tell Cherylanne good-bye. Then I think, again, how can he *sleep*? I pick up my suitcase, go to stand beside his open bedroom door. "Dad?" I whisper. The shades are drawn; his room is purple black. "Good-bye," I whisper. And then, "It's all right."

*D*ickie is waiting outside, and he is surprised to see me, I can tell, though he is trying to make his face mainly polite. "Hey, look who's coming," he says, and then, to Diane, "Is she?" Diane nods, hoists my suitcase, then hers into the back of his truck. "Go ahead, get in," she tells me, and I guess that I am to sit in the middle, just like I imagined. Everything they say to each other will have to pass over me. I can stay quiet as can be and still be in the conversation. I get in, Diane gets behind the wheel, and Dickie goes to the back of the truck. At first I think he is walking away, giving us the truck. But then Diane shifts into neutral, nods at him, and he begins to push. A silent leave-taking. This must be how they've done it before. I hold my breath until we are a good block away. Then Diane stops the truck and hops out to move to the other side. Dickie gets in and starts the engine. We are going. And in his bed, he is sleeping.

*O*nce I got into bed with him and my mother. I was sick, full of longing for the feel of someone else's normal flesh, and so I crawled in beside her. She awakened instantly, felt my forehead, and got up to get me something. "Don't wake your father," she said.

I lay still and listened to him breathe. There was a smell to him that I felt in my nose and in my throat. He was wearing a T-shirt on top; I didn't know what on the bottom. I took in a ragged breath, closed my eyes, opened them. I could see the green glow of their alarm clock, hear a muffled, rapid tick. Where was my mother? He stirred then, reached out, and lay a heavy arm across me. I jumped, thinking he'd been going to hit me, and the movement must have awakened him. "What are you doing here?" he said. "What happened?"

"I'm sick," I said, and then, "Mom said to wait here."

"What's wrong with you?"

I shrugged. "I don't know."

He felt my forehead. "You have a fever."

"Yes."

"Does anything hurt?"

"Just my throat. And my ears. And some in my stomach."

"That's a lot to hurt."

"Well, only a little in my stomach."

"All right." He turned over, went back to sleep.

He doesn't like people to talk about pain. Once he had to have an operation on his stomach. He never said anything about it—not before and not during and not after. When we went to the hospital to visit him, I saw him from outside his door before he saw us. His face was like before you have to make a big jump across something deep. Then when he saw Diane, my mother, and me, he changed into normal. He nodded and said to give him his robe, and he sat up and said he was taking us to the hospital cafeteria. And he did, walked slowly beside us in his paper slippers. His face was sick white and he was pushing a pole with a big bottle swaying on it. I got french fries and Diane got an ice cream sandwich and my mother got tea and he said, no, he didn't want anything, he wasn't allowed to have anything, but he paid. I was glad to see his same old wallet in his robe. He watched us eat and then he went back to his room and got into bed and told us to go home. Before we left, he called my mother back. "Lock the windows," he said. "Check the basement before you go to sleep."

"I love you," she said, and bent down to kiss his cheek. He stared straight ahead, nodded. After she turned to leave, I saw him pull one hand up slowly over his stomach, then the other. In school the next day, I cried thinking about it. I said it was because I had a headache, and I got to go home. My mother put me on the sofa under the afghan, brought me tomato soup with crackers crumbled on top, and looked at the Sears catalog with me. What I wanted—a red lawn mower, circle-stitch brassieres, a canopied bed—I circled in black. What she wanted—an electric dryer, new carpeting, and a yellow V-necked sweater, she circled in blue. All in all, it was worth it to lie.

For a while when I was younger, I used to pretend-run-away all the time. I would dump my doll out of her suitcase and use it to pack all my underwear in, and go far into a field that was behind the house we lived in then. There I would sit on a big rock and contemplate the distance around me in four directions. I would listen to the buzzing insects, make up ideas for new parents. Mostly they were tall and slender. She had long red hair with a wave over one eye. He had short blond hair and wore a blue blazer with a family crest. They had many kinds of drinking glasses and two servants. "Look at her!" they would say, introducing me to their astonished and jealous friends. "Lost, can you imagine! Turns out she's real intelligent, too. Why, we just took her right in! Of course it helps that we're millionaires, but we would have taken her even if we didn't have one red cent." I'd heard that phrase, "one red cent," and it appealed to me. I used it whenever I could.

I never went any farther than the rock. I would sit for a while and then go home. My mother would give me peaches from the can and then together we would put away my underwear. "I'm so glad you're home," she would say. "Shall we read a little?" I knew not to let my father catch me running away, even if it was pretend.

And now it is not pretend. It is so real we have a truck and the driver is drinking coffee. Later I might get scared about what will happen when my father finds out. But now there is wide-open night outside the rolled-up windows, the road passing under the two front tires of the truck and out from under the two rear ones. Imagine if I fell out, I think suddenly, and had to watch the taillights get smaller in the dark. Imagine if I had to be all alone somewhere far from anywhere—Texas is scary vast. But I am in the middle, where I couldn't fall out without someone taking notice. I close my eyes, listen to the drone of the tires on the pavement. It is a high song, and it can hypnotize you in that way where you just can't move your eyeballs even though you know you are awake. I like when you know you're going to fall asleep any second. That is the time for the last thoughts of the day to come into your brain like the

tail end of a long parade. It's colors I think of tonight: the corals you see on seashells, the swirls of
white through pink on Cherylanne's lipstick holder,
the shy blue of the sky when the day is coming new.

I wake up to the crunch of gravel. Dickie has
pulled into the parking lot of The Welcome Inn.
Well, the "W" is off the "Welcome," but what else
could it be? It is light outside, but gray, the clouds
hanging low and swollen above us. The motel looks
like a shoe box, long and narrow with about twelve
doors leading to different rooms. The doors are
painted yellow, red, green; yellow, red, green. I hope
we get a red one. Diane is sound asleep, her head
resting against her window. Dickie smiles at me,
whispers, "I'll be right back," and heads for the room
on the end with a sign saying OFFICE leaning against
its window. A motel room! For all of us! In the
daytime! Already we are making up our own rules
for whatever we want. After we get going again, I'll
bet if I want to stop and look at something, Dickie

and Diane will say, "Why certainly. Go ahead." We could never do that before. My father drove and drove and we couldn't look at anything even if my mother asked. Once she begged him to let us see a cave only one mile off the road. He was quiet for one terrible moment and then he turned to her and said between his teeth, "I am trying to *get* there. Could you please make some effort to understand that? I am not interested in side trips. I am interested in getting there." Her earring jiggled a little from her starting to turn toward him. But then she stopped, just looked down, I'm sorry.

She packed a freezer chest with food for us. We ate ham sandwiches and slices of pie and potato chips and apples. We fought noiselessly, and every time we slept it was like a miracle, because we weren't tired at all, we were ready to bust out of our skins from plain boredom. But we couldn't stop, except for every four hours to pee and fill up the gas tank.

I hear the rumble of thunder and think how perfect it will be to sleep now, while it rains. Then I remember how my father never uses an umbrella. "Customs of the service," he once told me, and showed me in *The Officer's Guide* where it said, "There is a long-standing Army taboo against an officer in uniform carrying an umbrella." I thought that was so queer I learned it by heart right then. My father doesn't have a single question about it. He never uses an umbrella out of uniform, either. He stands straight up in the rain and lets it have him. Little streams of water slide down his face, into his eyes, down his neck, and under his shirt. Remembering this, something inside me takes an elevator to the next floor down. I don't know why I get sorry for him this way. All of a sudden, I just do.

Of course he will be all right without us. Nancy Simon can cook him dinner in her own aprons, which probably look stupid. Maybe he will get truly sad sometimes, drop his face in his hands, and say, "Oh, I have gone and lost my children." But Nancy will lay his roast beef on his plate, saying, "Now, now. What's done is done," and kiss him with her greasy lips. She will not do anything right, and I only hope he will notice.

I cannot sleep. For one thing, I am on the
floor. It is the fair place; there is only one bed. Dickie
volunteered to let Diane and me sleep there, but
Diane said no. She said, "You don't mind the floor,
do you?" but it wasn't really a question. She was a
little sorry, but she is shaping her new life and she
figured she might as well get going.

The floor is hard, of course, but that is not the
problem. One problem is that there is a chemical
smell to the carpet, mixed with cigarette smoke, and
the combination is about to kill me. I am breathing
through my fist over my nose. Also, the air conditioner is leaking. I can hear drops of water, see a fat
stain spreading out on the wall. Another problem is
that Dickie is snoring so loud that at first I thought
he was just kidding around, trying to make me
laugh. But he's not kidding; he's sound asleep and I
guess Diane is, too. I've been watching her and she
hasn't moved even to turn over. I guess she stayed
awake with him until the end. But I fell asleep
almost as soon as we left, and I am done sleeping.
Every time I close my eyes my body gets nervous,

like I'm making a big mistake and it had better let me know. My eyelids jerk right back open like a Laurel and Hardy windowshade. The day is trying to get around the pulled-shut drapes; the world is in the go position.

I get up and quietly open the desk drawer. If there is some paper, I'll write a letter to Cherylanne. "Guess where I am!" it will begin. But then I realize I don't know where I am. There is no paper, anyway. There is only a brown book, with *Holy Bible* written in gold across the front.

I flip open to a page where Jesus is giving another speech. Everything He says is in red. I used to like Jesus. I thought He knew me. When I took communion, I believed that as long as the wafer was in my mouth, Jesus was in my heart. He was in my heart miniature but whole, with His own heart lit up and exposed and circled with roses and thorns. His arms were outstretched and His eyes were raised upward, which meant he was paying serious attention to me. I could speak with Him one-on-One, for as long as I could make the wafer last. The fact that other people had wafers made no difference: they had other arrangements. I was careful not to move my tongue against the wafer, which was lodged against the roof of my mouth, except for rare times when I really didn't have much to say. Then I would release Him early. After all, He was busy. People everywhere were calling Him in languages you never heard of, night and day. But I asked Him to let me keep my mother, and He said no, and so I had no more interest in Him.

I put the Bible back, shut the drawer, take an eyeball tour of the room. A double bed, brown-and-orange-striped bedspread, and iron-smell sheets. Two pillows, no extra—I used Dickie's jacket for my pillow. A high, narrow rectangle of a window. A small desk below it. An orange chair in the corner, wooden arms. A nightstand and there you are, that is it. Oh, and a closet, small, with a few lonely hangers, not new.

I tiptoe into the bathroom. Here is a tub and a sink and a toilet that comes with a break-away paper band that makes you feel like the Queen of Sheba, even if the toilet is five hundred years old. There are white towels and little bars of soap stacked up, enough so we can each have our own. Well, I could wash. I open a soap, smell it, turn on the water slow

and quiet. I wash my face and hands, dry off, fold up
the towel, wrap up the soap. Then I tiptoe to my
suitcase, get my pen, and go back to the bathroom to
write my name on my soap wrapper. I will use the
soap here, then bring along what's left. We will need
soap. I look into the mirror for a while. I wish I'd
brought a nail file. Cherylanne always carries one in
her purse. In a nothing-to-do emergency, she will
pull it out and get to work.

I go out into the room and sit in the orange
chair, watch them sleep. I am a little hungry. Where
will we eat? I wonder. Probably at a restaurant with
booths, and place mats with stars for cities. Who has
money? I think only Dickie does.

I get out my poetry notebook, close my eyes,
and wait for an idea. Sometimes they are swirled
around in there deep, and I have to tell them they
can come out. But nothing comes to me. *A*, I think.
Nothing. *B. C.* Nothing. *D. E. Eternity. Eternity.* I
write:

I hate eternity.
Really, friend, don't you?

What could stay good so long?
Not even a great zoo.

Well, this is silly.
I write:

Think of how long
Eternity can last

Nothing. I take in a breath, sigh, then worry that it is too loud. I'll go outside. I don't like to think about eternity. It scares me. It's like a too-tight winter muffler, acting like it's there to help you when all it's doing is cutting off your breathing. What *could* you do for so long? Sometimes when I think of heaven, I think all it is is people looking down and missing things. And if God came walking through and said, "Anybody want to go down there again?" everybody would raise their hand yes, even if their time here had been hard.

I open the door. The rain has stopped, the sun is out, and the slice of day that leaks in falls directly on Diane's face. She opens her eyes, crabby. Well, there is nothing to do about it now. "I'm going out,"

I say, and she frowns, nods, turns over on her other side.

I guess I have messed up. I will make it up to her later. But who could sit in a small dark room that is not your own, with nothing but two people sleeping, and you don't know for how long?

There is a small swimming pool in front of the motel. No one is in it. I wish I'd brought a suit, but of course I didn't know you could go swimming when you are running away. I open the gate, go sit by the edge of the pool to hang my feet in. The water feels cool and fine, like liquid silk. I close my eyes, spread out my toes, make the pool bigger in my mind to feel more luxurious.

I won't get to go to the pool anymore with Cherylanne. The last time, I didn't know it was the last time. I should have paid more attention. The best was our diving, how good we got at back dives. Of course, I never did learn the high dive. I see Cherylanne coming off it, one smooth letting go. She often smiled when she dived; I wonder if she knew it. I see myself back up on that high board, and hairs on the back of my neck rise up to remember it too.

My father must know by now. He must have

seen our empty rooms. Maybe he looked for me at Cherylanne's. "I don't know!" Cherylanne would say and he would not quite believe her, probably. Belle would have to come, put her arm on Cherylanne's shoulder, say, "She was here last night, and then this morning she was gone. We don't know anything more about it than that."

He would go home, mad. He would sit in his chair, think, I'm going to let them both have it this time. I shiver, pull my feet out of the water. They shouldn't sleep too long. Only enough to be able to drive again. We can sleep in Mexico for a thousand hours.

I get up, take a walk around the parking lot. There is a restaurant across the highway. I'll have cereal. Maybe some eggs if they're cheap. I'll walk around the building slow fifteen times. If they're not up, I'll go make some noise in there.

On my tenth time around, a man comes out of the office and asks if can he help me. "Oh, no," I say. "I'm just getting some exercise."

He nods, looks at me like maybe I am crazy. But then he just goes back inside the office. I follow him. "Do you need any help?" I ask.

"Pardon me?"

"Is there anything I can help you with?"

He waits, opens his mouth, closes it. Then, "What unit are you in?"

"Seven," I say. "A green one."

"I think you'd better go back there," he says.

Well, now I have messed up twice. He could get suspicious. I could wreck everything. I will go back inside, sit quiet until they get up. I can play checkers in my head.

I open the door and Diane rolls over again. "Close it!" she whispers, hard. I close it and she gets up, points to the bathroom. I go in and she follows me. "What the hell are you doing?" she says. "We've been up all night! You need to be quiet."

I nod, look away from her at my soap. That was from when everything was going fine.

"What's the matter with you?" she asks.

I shrug. "I don't know. I'm not tired."

She sighs, looks away, then back at me. "I'll give you some money," she says. "You can get something to eat. There's a restaurant across the highway."

"I know," I say. And I want to add all the other

things I know are here: many varieties of weeds. Wildflowers, purple and pink and yellow. All the same kind of yellowish rock. One horny toad, at least. It takes forty steps to walk along the front and the back of the building, ten to get past the side. I guess I know there is a restaurant across the highway. I guess I don't need Diane to tell me.

She goes out of the bathroom, comes back with her purse, hands me a fiver. "Be careful crossing," she says.

"Do you want anything?" I ask.

"Yes. Sleep."

"Okay."

I go outside, sit by our door. I don't want to eat alone. I'll wait until I'm too hungry to be scared of it. And then I'll eat slow. For now, I'll just watch whatever happens. Or doesn't.

*W*e are on the road again, and I am sitting in the back of the truck. There's some privacy here. Nobody is la-de-dah minding you. I can't wait for this day to be over because it is nothing but bad. I ate a candy bar for breakfast, because I sure wasn't going to sit in that restaurant alone. All the tables full of people sitting together, kids playing with their straws and talking a mile a minute, adults drinking coffee and smiling at them, *Aren't you cute?* The hostess dressed in her puffy sleeves and little hat asking me, "Can I help you?" her eyes squinty with suspicion. Well, I just said no thank you, and went over to the vending machine. I got some change and bought a Nestle's Crunch. I ate it by the pool and then I sat outside the motel room until they were ready to go. Dickie came out first, smiling and sleepy, and I was not in the mood to try to come up with something, so I didn't say anything. He and Diane went to get coffee and I said, "Oh, no, I just ate," and then I had to wait some more. I might as well have been Chinese-tortured. I made the bed in the motel room. I opened the drapes all the way. I dusted the tabletops with some toilet paper. And then they came back, Diane put the suitcases in the truck, and Dickie spread the map across the hood. Here was the dangerous part, with all of us thinking, Can he find us?

And now we have passed through Beeville on our way to Corpus Christi. The ocean is there, I know. Diane wants to live near the ocean, but in Mexico, and so naturally that is just exactly where Dickie is taking her. I knock on the rear window. It's hot; I want back in the truck. Dickie slows, pulls over to the side of the road, and I climb in the middle.

"Did you get burned?" Diane asks.

I shrug. She must have been struck blind: I believe I look like Crayola violet-red.

"We'll stop for lunch soon," Diane says.

"Okay."

She turns to look out the window. Silence. This happens when you travel. First everyone talks a lot, then a little, then only the road talks. We haven't stopped to look at anything. We are just getting away.

"Armadillo," Dickie says, pointing to the side of the road. It is dead, lying on its side, a sick cloud of flies above it. At their dirt home, I think of Mrs. Armadillo saying to her children, "Where could he be?"

By now my father has called the MPs, probably the civilian cops, too. "Find my daughters," he has told them, and they have said, "Yes, sir." When they leave, he walks around the house. I know the walk. I know the eyes. I look behind us. Off in the far distance, one other truck. Black. Nothing else.

Dickie slows the truck, starts pulling over to the side. There is a man hitchhiking there. He comes up to the window and Dickie nods at him. "Need a lift?" The man nods back, grateful.

"Back of the truck okay?"

"Fine with me," the man says, and climbs in. He is old, and I wonder what he is doing hitching. Anyone can end up any way.

"I'll go in back, too," I say. Dickie looks at Diane. She leans over to look at the old man, shrugs all right.

I climb out, get into the back of the truck. "Hi," I say, and the truck pulls out onto the highway.

The man extends his hand. "Theodore Bender."

"I'm Katie," I say. No last names. He could turn us in.

"Where y'all headed?" he asks.

"Oh, just out for a ride," I say.

The man nods.

"Don't you have a car?" I say.

"Nope. Nor a house neither."

"Oh." I look out at the flatness we're passing through. The sky is deep blue, empty of the variety of clouds. The man stretches out, puts his head on his backpack.

"I never have liked to be in one place only," he says. "I like to keep moving. I do a few odd jobs, move along. You should stay out of the sun, little lady." He closes his eyes. We are done talking. I had hoped for more. This trip is not turning out right one bit. All I have gotten everywhere are bad signs.

When Dickie pulls into a restaurant parking lot, the man wakes up. "Guess this is my stop," he says, and winks at me. Then he goes to the road and sticks his thumb out again. When will he decide to stop? I wonder. What will say to him, this is the place. When I come into our kitchen, it's the dish rack I always look at first. The pots and pans always lie slanted on top of the plates and bowls; the silverware always stands up in neat rows; the dish towel always hangs folded on its circular hanger. But sometimes you don't know what it is that tells you

you are in the right place; there is just a kind of lying down of your insides, a message from yourself to relax, you are home.

I am suddenly very tired.

The restaurant tables are all lined up against the window. There are red-and-white tablecloths, and groupings of salt, pepper, and sugar all huddled together like family. The menus are old and good looking. I ask for a burger and fries and I can't wait to get them. Dickie gets chicken-fried steak and Diane gets a BLT. Cokes all around.

When the waitress leaves, I can see we are all in a good mood, the way ordering food makes you get. Well now, you think, your hands folded on the table. I am taken care of. All I do is wait now.

Dickie looks out the window at the old man, who is still asking at the side of the road for a ride. "Wonder who he is," he says.

"He does odd jobs, and then he moves on," I say.

Dickie smiles. "What a life."

"I think I'd like it," Diane says. "I do! Never stay anywhere."

"You don't like to move all the time," I say.

"I don't like somebody else telling me where to move," she says. "But if I could decide when and where, I'd like to move around."

"Not me," I say. I shift in my seat. Sometimes I forget how different we are. Diane never liked dolls. She doesn't like to read. She can watch a sad movie like *Imitation of Life*, where I saw even GIs crying, and only say, "That was stupid!" at the end.

I excuse myself to go to the rest room. I pass by a phone booth and it is empty, the door open. I go in and close the door, lean my head against the cool glass. A little fan is whirring and an overhead light has come on. We are open for business. I know how to do it. You dial *O*, say, "Make this collect."

I close my eyes, think of my old life. And when I see my things in my room, they lean forward to call me back. I think of Cherylanne, how when she sits on the low back porch her knees go together while mine go apart, and I wonder is she lying on her bed reading magazines, with hurt feelings.

I put a dime in, dial *O*. I tell the operator I want to make a collect call, and I give her Cherylanne's number. Cherylanne answers and I hear her asking Belle, "Can we accept a collect call?" Then there is Belle on the line saying yes, she will accept, and then, "Katie, for God's sake, where are you, honey?"

"Oh, I'm with Diane," I say.

"Where?"

"Well, we're on our way somewhere."

Belle's voice gets low and serious. "Katie, your father is very upset."

I want to hang up. I have made a big mistake.

"Just one minute!" I hear Belle telling Cherylanne. And then, back to me, "Katie, honey, you need to come home. Can you tell me where you are?"

"I don't think so."

"Can you just tell me where you are?"

I swallow.

"Katie?"

"Can I talk to Cherylanne?"

She sighs. I hear her muffled voice tell Cherylanne to give her back the phone when we are through.

"Where are you?" Cherylanne asks. "Did you run away?"

"Yes."

"Oh my God."

"So. What are you doing?"

"Katie, you can't do this. This is not right. Your father is really mad."

"What did he do?"

"He came looking for you, of course. And *I* didn't know where you went. When did you leave?"

"It was late. I don't know."

"You'd better come back. This is not right."

Well, I am getting annoyed. How does she know what is right? "I told you I was leaving," I said. "You never did believe me. But here I am."

"Where are you?"

I look out at Dickie and Diane. Our food has come. They can't see me in here. "I am pretty far away," I say.

"Where?"

I wait, then say it. "Bayside. At a restaurant called Jenny's. It's on Highway 80. I don't think you should tell."

"Should we come and get you?"

And there it is.

"Should we come and get you, Katie?"

I hang up.

I go to the bathroom, wash my face. I am

burned a sorry red, all right. My skin will fall off later, like dandruff. I dry off carefully with a paper towel that feels like steel wool. I go back to the table, sit down. I'm not hungry anymore. You would think someone would notice my burn.

"There's your burger," Diane says.

I nod, pick up a french fry, put it back down. Diane stops chewing. "What?" she says.

"I think I'll go home," I say.

Her eyes widen. "Did you call him?"

"No. But I think I'll go home."

"Jesus!" She is angry-hurt. "Jesus!"

"Take it easy, Diane," Dickie says. "Lower your voice."

"I'll bet she called him!" Diane says.

"Did you?" Dickie asks.

"No," I say. And then, "Cherylanne. I called her."

Diane stands up, grabs her purse. "Well, that's it. He's on his way. Let's get the hell out of here."

Dickie sighs. "Look, Diane. He won't be here for hours. Eat your food."

She sits back down, stares at me. "Why'd you

do that? I'm trying to help you. What do you want, to go back and live with him?"

Oh, the answer is sorrowful to me, too.

We make the arrangements: they will leave. I will wait on the bench just outside the restaurant. Before they pull away, Diane hugs me. She's hardly ever done that. I don't know her smell. "When we get to Mexico, I'll write you," she says. "Okay?"

"Okay."

"Don't you leave here, no matter how long it takes, okay? This place is open twenty-four hours; someone will be here all the time."

"Okay."

She is desperate looking, suddenly, and I feel sorry for her. "What will you do?" she asks.

"I'll just wait," I tell her. "I have a good imagination."

She hugs me again, and there is a kiss on my hair. And then the truck pulls away and she is gone.

I sit in the shade and chart the progress of the clouds. Later, I will eat again. I have a twenty-dollar bill in my pocket from Dickie. Diane is right: he is a good man. Picks up hitchhikers. Gives out money. Takes a woman wherever she wants to go.

*H*e brings the puppy. When he gets out of the car, he is holding her. She is wearing a little red leash and a collar. She stops to pee when he puts her down, and he is standing there holding onto the leash, and I walk up to him slow.

"Where is Diane?" he asks.

"She went on. She's with Dickie."

He nods. "Do you know where she went?"

"Mexico. She doesn't want to come back."

No words. The space between us nearly solid. "Would you please get in the car now?"

"Okay." I come closer, take the leash from his hand. "You brought Bridgette," I say.

He nods. "Nobody to watch her."

*H*e can drive for hours and hours, it doesn't bother him. All he would ever ask is for my mother to rub his neck, get after the stiffness. He could go sixteen hours easy. I sit in the front for a while, then go to lie down on the backseat. When I wake up, dark is coming. I sit up, rub my face. The puppy is awake in her box, her two paws lined up neat in front of her like she is ready for inspection. "I think we should stop and let this puppy run around a little," I say.

He says nothing.

"Dad?"

"Maybe later."

"I think she needs out now, though. Could we just pull over?"

He puts on the turn signal, pulls over. We take the puppy out, let her sniff. He stretches, rubs his neck. I let the puppy run, give her a stick to carry. "Where are we?" I ask.

"Not so far," he says. "Couple more hours."

He sits down on the ground and I sit beside him. "I'm sorry."

"Yeah." He sighs.

I pick up the puppy, put her in my lap, but she wants down, so I let her. I let the silence be, too. Occasionally a car passes. There are grasshoppers here, leaping up all crazy about something every now and then. I am wondering what they eat, when I hear my father speak softly.

"Pardon?" I ask.

He turns to me. "I was talking about your mother."

"Oh."

"I know how much you miss her."

"You do?"

"Oh, yes. She was . . . There's nobody like her."

"I know."

"Her disease started out in one place, but then it just went everywhere. Nothing in her body could work right anymore. What killed her . . ." He stops, and I am careful not to move. Finally, he says, "What killed her is that she couldn't breathe anymore." He is saying this like the teacher called on him and he is giving the answer anyone would know. Silence. A car goes by, kicks up a piece of gravel that flies toward us, lands at my father's feet.

I would say I saw it and didn't. "I want you to know she died peacefully, Katie."

There.

"She talked about you and Diane before she died."

And there.

He looks away from me, shakes his head. Then he turns back and sighs. "Okay?"

I nod quick.

"I don't . . . I don't think I'd ever like to talk about it again, Katie, okay? But you deserved to know. I should have told you when you asked."

I stand up, lead the puppy along on her leash. I guess she believes she is in a New York City parade: her step is high, her ears are swinging flirty. Not many people know about dogs' moods, but I do. "She walks good," I say.

"Yes. She'll be a fine dog, I guess."

"We should go home, Dad."

He is quiet for the rest of the way. All he says is "Here we are" when we get home. Then he goes into his bedroom and closes the door, and so do I. All my things, eager. I lie on my bed, then slide under it. I think, what happened? Well, I learned that the rest of the world is closer than I thought. There's that. I cry a little, but mostly I only get peaceful. She would rub my back when I cried. She would say, "Oh, now. Look at this. Oh, my. Oh, dear. Yes, I know." She knew the short little words to grief.

*C*herylanne and I go swimming the next day. I have everything back for a little while and I am so grateful. I memorize the light that bounces off the water. I study the bones in Cherylanne's wrist. The towels that we lie on touch.

Paul Arnold comes up to us as we are drying off after the first swim. He has hair above his belly button in curly rows. "I heard you ran away," he says. I can see Cherylanne's lips tighten. Happy as she is to see me again, she can't stand that I am so interesting now.

"Yes, I did."

"With your sister?"

"Yes, and her boyfriend, Dickie. He has that truck?"

Paul nods.

"Well," I say, "it was pretty exhausting and dangerous. I'm actually glad to be home."

He nods. Say he was my husband: I would have told him about running away while we were in bed. He would have pulled me over, the crook of his arm a house for me. He would have had me say the good parts twice. I would feel low down how much he loved me. Low down and all around.

"We're having a water war," he says, interrupting my fantasy. "Want to be my partner?"

Ride on his shoulders while he walks around tough. The idea is to knock another girl off another boy's shoulders. I have never been asked.

"Okay," I say. And then, "Is there someone for Cherylanne?"

He shrugs. "Sure."

"I am tanning," she says, and closes her eyes snotty, but then when Bobby Simpson comes up to ask her to fight, she is on her feet in one second flat.

I unseat three girls, but not Cherylanne. When we come up against each other, neither one of us tries. At the end, it is the two of us and we say we both win. Then we all go to the snack bar together, two boys, two girls, and I guess I have had a date. We are moving in three days, but it all counts.

On the last day, after the moving van has gone, I walk around the empty house. There are marks on the walls, evidence of how we were. It is the loneliest thing, to see those last pieces of you that stay behind. I go into the laundry room, remember her ironing and folding. In the kitchen I turn the water on and off, open and close a cupboard door. I hear, "Kaaaatie!" Dinnnnner!" and I whisper, "Coommming!" I push shut a partially open drawer. The sound echoes off the walls.

I walk through the living room, which is bigger-seeming now. I am standing by the door when it opens and Cherylanne comes through it. She has been crying, and so of course this starts me in, too. We hug each other, make our little sob sounds together. It is a comfort to me that she feels so bad. "I brought you something," she says, finally, and pulls out a small gift from behind her back. I open it, find an all-in-one makeup kit. Even Cherylanne doesn't have this. There is miniature everything: shadow, mascara, lipstick, liner, blush, all in a beautiful shiny black box with a mirror on the inside lid. "Oh, thank you," I say. "Did you get one, too?"

"No," she says, shaking her head, her eyeballs glued to the kit. "Not yet. And I'm waiting a good week to get one, in your honor."

"Well," I say. "Thank you."

"Will you write me?" she asks, and her voice is shaky sad again.

"Of course," I say.

"Maybe you could send me some poems."

"Well," I say, "you never liked them before."

"I know," she says, and pulls out a lace-trimmed hanky to dab at her nose. "But now they will be mailed."

"Oh," I say. "That's right."

"Well," she says, and sighs big. "I hate this part."

"Me, too."

"Okay. So—have a good trip and write me. Every day."

"I will."

"And I will, too."

"Okay."

"Okay." She shrugs, goes to the door, turns back. " 'Bye."

I watch her going back home, and though the distance is very short, she runs. "Shut up, Bubba!" I hear her yell. He must have made fun of her crying. I wipe my eyes.

I go upstairs, walk past my father's empty bedroom, mine, the bathroom, then come to the closed door to Diane's room. I open it and see him in there, just standing in the middle of the emptiness. "Ready?" he asks, as though he has come in and found me.

"I guess."

"Okay."

I look at his hands in his pockets. I believe he has put something in there, something he found in Diane's room. I wonder what it is. But I won't ask him. It is his. He looks around, scans the ceiling, the floor, the walls. I take him by the hand and lead him out.

*W*e have gone one hundred miles. We are going to go five hundred, he said. I see a billboard for A&W. One half mile up the road, turn right, go three hundred yards. "Look!" I say. "Can we stop?"

He shakes his head no. "I want to make time, Katie."

I turn around to check on Bridgette. She is lying quietly, her nose on her paws, thinking. She is a good traveler. She doesn't know she's going to live in Missouri.

I turn back, say quietly, "We could just get one root beer float."

"Did you hear me, Katie? What did I just say? What did I *just say*?" His voice is louder, on its way up. Now is where you must be quiet for a good ten minutes and let him cool off. It is better not to move anything on your body either. Invisible.

And yet. "This could be the last A&W in the whole world, with everything on sale today only," I hear myself say.

He sighs, slows down, and puts on the turn signal. Well, I certainly know not to say thank you.

What must it be like, I think, driving out of Texas, in the opposite direction from your other daughter? Whatever he is feeling is letting him get me a root beer float, I know that. We see the A&W, a good big one.

"I thought Diane was the one crazy about A&W," he says.

"No. It's me, too."

"Okay."

We crunch in over the gravel and find a spot. "Two root beer floats," my father tells a silver speaker, then adds, "And a burger, plain." He looks at me, shrugs. "For the dog."

I roll my window down all the way, lean my elbow out. It's hot, the float will taste good. I realize suddenly that I am seated in my own place. This air, and the air around me, is mine, I know now. I look at my father, see Diane lost in his face, his own true regret. I feel some part of him come into me as though there were a thin wire connecting us, heart to heart, with all that must most be said translated into barely visible vibrations. I see his leg, see his bent knee, remember the times when I got to sit in the front for a while, between my mother and him. He would occasionally reach out to give me a horse bite. It hurt a little, but it tickled, too. I would look up at him, ready for my part, but he stared straight ahead, not acknowledging himself. He can only go so far in a good direction. Then something happens. He is all apart broken. For a moment I see him as someone other than my father, and he seems so curious to me, and sad, like an animal wrongly tied up. Then he is my father again and I see that he is only what I was given first. There are other places to look for things. I lean back against the seat, close my eyes.

I am back on the diving board, small against the night sky. The board is much higher now, silvery in the moonlight. And I walk toward the end of it, three steps, bounce high, point myself toward the water. I feel my hair straighten in the wind; it is such a long way down. I feel the cool night air against my body the most just before I enter the water. For a long time, I am propelled downward toward the bottom of the pool, but then all I do is arch my back, change direc-

tion, kick my feet once, hold my body straight, and let myself rise up.

I hear the inviting rattle of glasses, smell the hamburger. And now there is my father's voice, his hand lightly touching my arm. "Hey, wake up," he is saying. "Everything is here."

Durable Goods

Elizabeth Berg

A Reader's Guide

To print out copies of this or other
Random House Reader's Guides, visit us at
www.atrandom.com/rgg

Questions for Discussion

1. *Durable Goods* is a first-person narrative. What effect does this technique have on the telling of the story for you? Who is the novel's narrator, and what are some characteristics of her narrative voice? How does Berg's writing capture or evoke the character of adolescence?

2. Throughout the story, Katie sometimes calls her father "Dad," but most often refers to him as "he" or "him." It is clear that Katie and her sister are talking about their father, even though they never mention his name. Likewise, their mother also remains nameless throughout the novel. What does this tell you about Katie's relationship with her father and the evolution of her relationship with her mother?

3. Katie's father is a conflicted character. Though he is abusive and neglectful, he is not com-

pletely villainized. Discuss Berg's characterizations of Mr. Nash, as a man and as a father. How did you feel about him at the end of the book? Were you ever sympathetic toward him, as Katie becomes at the end of the novel, when she recalls him standing out in the rain without an umbrella?

4. Katie is an astute and insightful observer of people and situations. At one point she comments, "Sometimes, it seems to me that the only thing in the world is people just trying." How did you interpret this statement? How is this sentiment reflected in and woven throughout the novel?

5. There are several themes laced through the novel, such as the ways people cope with loss and grief and the different kinds of relationships between women. What are some of the underlying themes in this book, and how does Berg capture or express them? What literary techniques does she employ to convey the themes of the novel?

6. Discuss the title *Durable Goods*. Where is this phrase mentioned in the story, and what meaning does it hold for Katie? For her father? What meaning does it have for you?

7. The novel is shaded by a deep sense of spiritual-
ity. Katie speaks often of her relationship with
God, and we see how that relationship is affected
by the loss of her mother. How does Katie
reflect on religion? How does this help her cope
with a sense of grief?

8. Grief and loss are ongoing themes in the
book, on several levels. What sort of losses do
the Nash girls suffer throughout the book?
How do they cope with them? How does their
father cope with his grief? Give a few exam-
ples by which it becomes clear that communi-
cating pain is considered taboo in the Nash
household. What impact does this limitation
have on the relationships within the Nash
family?

9. Describe Katie's friend Cherylanne and her
family (Belle and Bubba). How does the appar-
ent disparity between the two girls and their
families help to shed light on Katie's character
and situation?

10. Berg's writing has been described as both
"quiet" and "delicate." With respect to *Durable
Goods,* how would you interpret these descrip-
tions? Do you think they are accurate? How
would you describe Berg's style in this novel?

11. *Durable Goods* is imbued with a sense of immediacy. How does Berg make the reader feel present in that particular time and place with Katie Nash? Select some passages that were particularly telling or successful in creating a sense of setting. Did Berg's technique in creating a literary atmosphere enable you to feel more connected to her characters?

12. While Katie's situation is unique, she is truly a universal character. Did you find yourself able to identify with her? If so, how, and at what points in the story did you feel most connected? Did you identify with any of the other characters? How?

13. The end of the novel is infused with both hope and sadness. Did the end of the book leave you wanting more or wondering what would happen to Katie, Diane, and their father? How did you feel about Katie's decision to return home? What do you predict will happen to the family at this point in their story?

Suggested Reading

Here, in no particular order, is a short list of books that I love. They focus on family, relationships, nature, domesticity, or childhood—or all of these at once. These are subjects I love to read and write about. You will find that in all of these books, the writing is outstanding. For me to love a book, I have to love the writing, first and foremost.

—*Elizabeth Berg*

One Hundred Demons by Lynda Barry
Ellen Foster by Kaye Gibbons
The Member of the Wedding by Carson McCullers
Caramelo by Sandra Cisneros
One Man's Meat (essays) by E.B. White
Ants on a Melon (poetry) by Virginia Hamilton Adair
A Christmas Story by Truman Capote
The Catcher in the Rye by J.D. Salinger
The Liars' Club by Mary Karr
An American Childhood by Annie Dillard
Places to Look for a Mother by Nicole Stansbury

200 *A Girl Named Zippy* by Haven Kimmel
     Anywhere but Here by Mona Simpson
     The Boys of My Youth (stories) by Jo Ann Beard
     Sweet Talk (stories) by Stephanie Vaughn
        (especially the story "Dog Heaven")
     Maus and *Maus II* by Art Spiegelman
     anything by Alice Munro